CHARLOTTE'S VOW

CHARLOTTE'S VOW

a novel by

MARION WOODSON

An imprint of
Beach Holme Publishing
Vancouver

First Edition

05 04 03 02 01 00 5 4 3 2 1

This book is published by Beach Holme Publishing, 226–2040 West 12th Avenue, Vancouver, B.C. V6J 2G2. This is a Sandcastle Book.

The publisher gratefully acknowledges the financial support of the Canada Council for the Arts and of the British Columbia Arts Council. The publisher also acknowledges the financial assistance received from the Government of Canada through the Book Publishing Industry Development Program (BPIDP) for its publishing activities.

The Canada Council | Le Conseil des Arts
for the Arts | du Canada

BRITISH
COLUMBIA
ARTS COUNCIL
Supported by the Province of British Columbia

Editor: Jen Hamilton
Production and Design: Jen Hamilton
Cover Art: Ljuba Levstek
Author Photograph: Clare Mosher

Printed and bound in Canada by Marc Veilleux Imprimeur

Canadian Cataloguing in Publication Data

Woodson, Marion.
  Charlotte's vow

  "A sandcastle book."
  ISBN 0-88878-413-9

  I. Title.
PS8595.O653C52 2000   jC813'.54   C00-910645-6
PZ7.W8685Ch 2000

For my grandsons: Charles, Thomas, Sam, Alec, Jake, and Evan

ACKNOWLEDGEMENTS

I wish to thank Jen Hamilton for exemplary editing, and Michael Carroll for wise counsel and unflagging attention to detail.

There is an old axiom that says books beget books, and that is certainly the case in this instance. Lynne Bowen's book *Boss Whistle* provided both the inspiration and the historical context for this novel.

ONE

It was Christmas 1912, and the younger McEwan children had been told that Santa Claus was having a few problems with his reindeer and wouldn't be able to bring any big presents. He did get there, though.

He left four-year-old Danny an orange, a whistle, a candy cane, and some new striped flannelette pajamas that had been made by Mrs. Santa Claus, of course.

"No, she didn't. She didn't sew them. Mummy did. I saw her the day before yesterday." Danny stuck his candy cane in his mouth and crossed his arms tightly over his chest.

"That's because Mrs. Claus didn't have time to finish them, so she asked Mother to do it, Danny-boy," Charlotte said as she scooped him up, hugged him, and pretended to nibble on his candy.

Charlotte, Robbie, and Beatrice each got an orange, a candy cane, and twenty-five cents. Charlotte tried to act surprised, although she had earned the money for the treats and the quarters herself looking after Mr. Trimble next door when his wife needed help now and then.

Mr. Trimble had broken his back in a mine accident and hadn't been out of bed for four years. They had seven kids, the Trimbles did, but they were lucky in some ways. They had a house to live in, free coal from the company, and a little money every month from relatives in England. They also kept a boarder. People wondered how they ever did it—ten people in a little company house—but Mr. Trimble didn't take up much room, and five of the kids slept in one bed. The boarder slept on a cot in the attic. It was cold in the winter and hot in the summer, but he was glad to find a place to stay at all.

The McEwans had a real upstairs with two small bedrooms under the gabled roof. The two boys slept in one, the two girls in the other. Their mother slept on a Winnipeg couch in the kitchen.

At noon that Christmas day they sat on wooden benches on either side of the kitchen table and ate roast grouse, potatoes with gravy, and mashed turnip. They admired the tree. It filled the house with the fresh scent of pine, and Beatrice discovered that, through half-closed eyes, the popcorn and cranberry garlands glowed against the dark green boughs.

They "fine-ly," according to Danny, opened the parcel from Scotland. There was a tartan scarf for each of the children, a silver-and-amethyst brooch in the shape of a thistle for their mother, and some special shortbread and toffee, which they ate for dessert. They all agreed it was just about the best Christmas dinner a family could wish for.

At two o'clock they got ready to go to the cemetery. Robbie didn't want to go. He was thirteen and considered himself the man of the family. "I'd better go pick some coal beside the tracks. Getting kinda low," he said in a pretty good imitation of a man's voice. Everybody could get cheap coal, but those who wanted to go and pick it up beside the train tracks or on the slag heap could get it for nothing.

Charlotte banked the stove and turned down the damper. The sweetish sulphury smell of burning coal was comforting. They would come home to a warm house.

Mabel McEwan opened the trunk where she kept her good clothes, lifted out her tweed coat, and put it on. She looked into a small mirror above the washstand as she adjusted her hat. Then she pulled on kid leather gloves, embroidered with a dark brown clover design across the backs, reached for a clean handkerchief from a shelf behind a flour-sack curtain, and tucked it into the top of one glove.

Charlotte thought that her mother was about the prettiest lady in Extension, when she wasn't overworried. She had thick auburn hair and dark brown eyes. She also had a way of suddenly becoming still in the midst of turmoil, as though she must listen for every nuance of sound with the intensity of a startled deer. What did she hear? Charlotte had often wondered, but she had learned long ago that her mother didn't have an answer to that question, or even seem to realize she was doing it.

There were a lot of single men in this coal-mining settlement, and many of them had eagerly offered, during the past three years, to take on the responsibility of the pretty widow and her children, but Mabel McEwan wouldn't give even one of them the time of day. She said she'd never marry another miner.

"Amen," Charlotte said.

They broke small branches from the Christmas tree, sent Robbie to fetch some Garry oak from a rocky bluff nearby, and gathered wild salal and Oregon grape from the tangle of undergrowth by the back fence.

Charlotte ran along the road, jumped over a ditch, and broke a single stalk from a snowberry bush. The slender branch with its clusters of waxy white berries was for her sister's grave.

Danny snapped off sprigs of Queen Anne's lace close to the dried brown seeds. "To bring to the senta-merry where Daddy and Janet are planted," he said.

"To the *cemetery* where Daddy and Janet are *buried*," Charlotte corrected him.

"I know that," Danny said indignantly.

The train that was used to transport miners to and from work was free to one and all that day, and it was noisy with the greetings and laughter of holidaymakers dressed in their finest.

The cemetery was in a little clearing behind the town of Ladysmith, and the McEwans placed their offerings on the graves. Danny divided his weeds into two separate bunches, then tossed them on top of the other tributes.

"That's nice, Daniel," his mother said. "Your father was always partial to wildflowers."

"Me, too," Danny said, whipping his whistle out of his pocket and blowing it before anyone could stop him.

"Hush. This is a cemetery. Act respectful now," his mother admonished.

The headstones were side by side:

4

Here lies George (Geordie) McEwan
Born Glasgow, Scotland, 1869
Died of afterdamp in
Extension Mine Explosion
October 5, 1909
Rest in Peace

Janet Louise McEwan
Born April 13, 1900
Died December 18, 1909
God Takes His Own

The year 1909 had been very bad. On October 4, empty clotheslines stretched across dreary backyards for the whole day. No washing out meant one of three things: it was Sunday, it was raining, or there was soot in the air. A fine dust of new snow sparkled in the sunshine on top of Mount Benson, but the little valley nestled below was hidden under a grey veil. In this pall of mist, smoke, and coal dust, the village of Extension went about its noisy business as usual. Trains shunted back and forth, the steam plant hissed to the accompaniment of drumming pistons, chunks of coal clattered into rail cars, and the mine bells rang.

In the afternoon women and children pumped pails of water, carried them into little houses identical to those of their neighbours, and poured the water into boilers on kitchen stoves to heat in preparation for the miners' homecoming baths.

The mine whistle signalled three short blasts, and underground, men—often soaking wet and always as black as the coal they mined—laid down their picks and shovels, picked up their lunch buckets, and waited for a ride to the top on one of the coal cars.

Mothers called to children, "Go and meet your father now." They ladled the warm water from the boilers into galvanized tubs, changed their aprons, stirred the beans, set the tables, and lit the coal-oil lamps.

In the morning the women packed double lunch pails: water or tea in the bottom compartment, sandwiches and cakes in the upper. The lunch pails never came home empty, and sometimes, if the worst happened, they never came home at all. Miners always saved a few swallows of drink, a crust of sandwich, a bite of cookie in case they were trapped underground.

After breakfast the men headed back to the pithead, down into the black tunnel.

At eight-thirty on the morning of October 5, the worst did happen. Ever after it was the haunting memory of the sounds that clutched at Charlotte's heart and made her throat ache. These sounds heralded death: the piercing siren and then the steady, low-pitched moaning of the mine whistle; the sobs of women; the whimpering cries of children; the loud, angry curses of men.

Hours later her father came out of the tunnel feet first on a coal car. His number was chalked on the sole of his boot. He looked perfectly normal, face and hands black with coal dust, cloth cap with a miner's lamp still attached lying beside him. One arm was flung across his chest as it often was when he slept. But he didn't move. The blackdamp did that to a man. No blood or broken bones or burned skin or water-filled lungs, but just as dead as those who came out all mangled and bloody.

The worst of it was that the disaster need not have happened. There was coal dust from a cave-in, and the fire bosses had reported it, but it wasn't that bad—so they said. The miners were using open lamps, and that did it. Safety lamps were a lot better, but they cost more. Thirty-two men, including Charlotte's father, died in the mine from an explosion and the poison gas that came after, because the company wouldn't spend money on better lamps.

Charlotte's next memory of that terrible time was of coffins being carried slowly up the hill to the beat of muffled drums and the mournful music of the "Dead March from Saul" played by the Silver Cornet Band. It took three days for the living miners to bury their dead comrades.

Charlotte knew many of these men, but they looked different, dressed in lodge regalia, their eyes sad, their voices husky. These black-clad strangers spoke quietly, shook her mother's hand, patted Danny's head.

"Don't worry about nothin', Miz McEwan, the lodge will take care of the expenses.... He was a good man, your Geordie was."

A dead husband and father meant no money. After the first rush of help—free coal, groceries, a few dollars from the other miners—they were on their own. The family then numbered six: Mabel McEwan, aged thirty-two; Charlotte, twelve; Robert, ten; Janet, nine; Beatrice, five; and Daniel, four months.

"Dry your tears now, Lottie. It's up to you and me to raise the little ones. It's a pity the house is not a mite bigger. We could have taken in a boarder, but the Lord does for them as do for themselves," her mother said to Charlotte the morning after her father's funeral.

"We'll manage to keep body and soul together. We'll let the word out that we'll pack lunches for them as needs it. We'll keep the little ones fed one way or the other." Mabel McEwan rarely showed any affection. "Being gushy," she called it when others talked about loving each other or hugged and kissed, except on very special occasions. Charlotte was surprised, therefore, when her mother put an arm around her shoulders, hugged her, and kissed her forehead. "We'll muddle through," she said.

"Muddling through" for Charlotte meant quitting school and doing laundry, scrubbing floors, and darning socks for other people. Sometimes, when a new baby was born, she was lucky enough to get a few weeks of steady housework at one place, for which she was paid nine dollars a month.

Then, only two months and twelve days later, it had been Janet, dead with pneumonia.

Sometimes Charlotte got the two deaths mixed up in her brain and imagined her father sweating and gasping for breath in the bed, and her little sister being brought out of the mine feet first. The mine had killed them both. Janet had not been a robust child, and breathing sulphury air laden with coal dust and smoke from the constantly burning fires on the slag heap had proved to be overwhelming odds against her struggle to live.

There were two things Charlotte was absolutely sure of: she would never marry a coal miner, and she would get a job as soon as she was old enough, save her money, and get herself and what was left of her family far, far away from coal mines.

Three years had passed since Charlotte's father had died, and more and more often she lay awake at night trying to figure out ways to keep her dream alive—not the one about never marrying a coal miner; she was sure that would be no problem—but the other part. How could she make enough money to get her family away from coal mines?

And now things were going from bad to worse. Some miners were out on strike, others were threatening to go, pro-union meetings often turned into shouting matches, and people didn't have money for extras, like help with child care and housework.

❦

"Beatrice! Get your clothes on this minute. Never in my born days have I seen such a dawdler. Lottie, will you give her a hand?" Mabel McEwan stirred the porridge, shook her head, and sighed.

"Come on, Bea, get a wiggle on. You'll be late for school," Charlotte said, pulling a black wool skirt over Beatrice's head. "You're eight years old. You should be able to get dressed by yourself. Beatrice! Pay attention." She bent down to stare into her sister's face.

Beatrice looked up dreamily. "Char...lotte?"

"Hmm?"

"Do you think if you could go up to the stars..."

"Don't be daft, Bea. Come on now, don't be a nuisance. Lift up your arms."

"But if you could, if you could go up to the stars, would it be all soft and floaty up there?"

"Crumbs, I don't know. Put on your stockings and shoes."

"Will you button my shoes, Lottie? Please? That's too hard a job for me."

"Yes, I'll button your shoes." Charlotte reached for the button hook and slipped small leather loops over the eight buttons on each of Beatrice's ankle-high boots.

"Eat your porridge now. There's a good girl." She ran up the stairs into the bedroom she and Beatrice shared, snatched a faded blue ribbon from the dresser post, ran down, and tied it around Beatrice's hair. "There. You look pretty as a picture, Bea."

"Wish I could get some new ones. Some girls at school have a different colour for every day. Ones for Sunday, and different ones for Monday, and everything." Bea lifted a spoonful of porridge and stared at it intently, as though watching multicoloured ribbons grow out of the mush.

"I'm going out for coal after school today," Robbie said with a jut of his chin.

"Oh, dear. I don't think you should do that, Robbie." His mother put a bowl of porridge in front of him. "Don't you be making a bother with the Chinese men now. We don't need more trouble in this house than we've already got."

"But they don't own the coal, no more'n we do. I'm doin' it and that's that. No son of a gun's goin' to beat me out of free coal."

"Robert! Watch your tongue!" Mabel jumped up to grab a dishrag as Danny's glass of milk tipped over.

"Sorr-ee, Mummie. I didn't mean to." Danny looked at her with his don't-be-mad-at-me-I'm-the-baby-in-the-family smile.

"I'm going to Nanaimo today," Charlotte announced. "I wish I could get a job." She stared dejectedly at the floor.

"Bide your time, Lottie. Your day will come." Her mother lifted Danny down from his chair, said "Go and play now," and sat down to her own porridge.

"Sure," Charlotte muttered. "So will a blue moon."

"What time?" her mother asked.

Charlotte raised her head. "What? I beg your pardon?"

"What time you planning to go to town? We had best wash clothes this morning. We've got a batch to do for the Flemings. I hope they can pay cash and not expect to give us eggs and such like for our trouble. He's on strike like the rest. Sun's going to shine, so we'd best get the washing done."

"All right," Charlotte said, lowering her head again. "I'll go this afternoon."

TWO

At last the white laundry had been boiled on top of the stove in empty kerosene cans, and the pit clothes had all been scrubbed on the washboard in the galvanized tub. Underwear, shirts, work pants, socks, pajamas, tablecloths, sheets, and towels were rinsed and hung, steaming, on the clothesline. Charlotte poured the dirty wash water on a dusty lilac bush in the yard. She was ready to leave.

"You won't be long, will you?" her mother asked. "Mrs. Trimble said she might want you for an hour around four. She has to take two of her children to the doctor."

"I'll be home by then. I'm going by Italy Town to see if Sophia wants to go."

The dirt road, full of muddy potholes and ruts, wound around boulders and four-foot-high stumps that had been left when timbers had been cut to prop up the mine shaft. Chimney smoke rose straight into the air, almost transparent in the watery sunshine. A rainbow arched above the mine, a false symbol of hope and promise. There would surely be more deaths in Old Number One. Already 373 men had died in mine explosions on Vancouver Island since the first mine opened in 1883.

Sophia Carpelli did want to go to town, but she spent forty minutes getting ready, and Charlotte began to regret stopping to ask her.

When Sophia finally emerged, Charlotte gasped. Her friend was dressed like a picture from the ladies' section of the Timothy Eaton catalogue. Her full-length coat, made of fine black melton cloth, was flared out slightly at the bottom. It had a fur collar and was fastened on the left side of the waist with one big fur button. Her hat was small with two jaunty peacock feathers, and she carried a fur muff.

"I just got clothes for Christmas. That's all I asked for. Do you like my hat?" she asked as they picked their way along the muddy road.

"Very becoming," Charlotte said with a quick nod. Her own homemade blue denim skirt, black wool stockings, and middy blouse under an olive-green cape felt heavy and boring beside Sophia's fashionable outfit. Even her new Christmas scarf didn't seem to be doing nearly as much for her morale as it had earlier.

Dowdy, that was the word for her, she said to herself.

"Don't you think the Trimbles' boarder is just too handsome for words?" Sophia asked.

"I guess so," Charlotte said. "He comes over and helps us, digs the garden, and fixes the shingles on the roof and such. But he stirs up trouble."

"How?"

"Oh, all this union business. He makes speeches and gets people all riled up. Mother says we have to be careful and not get overfriendly. All he can talk about is union, strike, and scabs and how rotten the company treats the men. But the company owns our house, and they could throw us out in a minute."

"Well, I think he's a catch. I'm going to set my cap for him," Sophia said with a laugh and a wink. "I'll take his mind off unions."

"Then he won't have a chance." Charlotte tried to match Sophia's mood, but her voice sounded flat and dull. Italians were so, so... They seemed to exaggerate everything. They were *so* happy, or *so* sad. They flung their arms about, and the women and girls walked down the road holding hands. A bit showoffish or something. Still, Charlotte wished she could be a little more like them. A little more "gushy," as her mother would say.

Sophia was two years older than Charlotte, and she thought she was the cat's meow. It didn't seem fair that she didn't have to worry about money, and she could get lisle stockings and new dresses practically whenever she felt in the mood. Her father was a fire boss and still working, even during the strike.

Sophia strutted and Charlotte trudged to the train stop. They went to the hospital to apply for jobs. Sophia filled out an application form, but Charlotte was too young. She had just turned fifteen, and she wouldn't be eligible for any job at the hospital, not even as a chambermaid, until she was sixteen.

The grocery and dry goods stores didn't need help. Neither did the newspaper or any of the hotels, the post office, the telephone company, or the movie theatres.

Later, after they had run out of jobs to apply for, they returned to Sophia's house, and Charlotte tried hard not to cry. It was all so discouraging.

"So, will you come?" Sophia asked.

"Huh? Come where?"

"To the theatre group. To join up. You're a good singer, and you used to get all the biggest parts at the school concerts because you could memorize so easily. How about it, Char? I'll come by your place around 6:30, okay?"

"I guess so."

"Good! See you later." Sophia turned with a flounce, unlatched the gate, and waved a suede-gloved hand as she stepped through.

＊

The Knights of Pythias Hall smelled of cedar wood, stale beer, cigarette smoke, and old coffeepots. Seven people were gathered near the stage. One young man handed out sheafs of paper.

"Here," he told them. "I sent all the way to Toronto for this. This is the new play. It sounds biffo. Just wait until you read it."

"It is," Mrs. Tweedsmuir said. "It's splendid. I adore Gilbert and Sullivan." Her husband was the boss at the dynamite plant, and they lived in a big house in Nanaimo. She was a proper lady and was related to a duke or some such person in England. People said Extension was lucky to have Olive Tweedsmuir come out and direct stage events in such a small community.

"Here he comes," Sophia whispered.

Charlotte looked toward the door. "Here who comes?"

"Shhh. The Trimbles' boarder. I hope he can sing. I want him for my leading man."

Sophia changed heartthrobs at the drop of a hat. She was always madly in love with somebody new, and Charlotte listened politely to her ravings about her latest beau, although frequently, Charlotte suspected, the man in question didn't know he was one.

Sophia winked at Charlotte as Jock Williamson walked toward them, his head turned so that he seemed to be studying the window curtains.

Jock doffed an imaginary hat. "Evening, ladies."

"And good evening to you, sir." Sophia had her hand out and was smiling up into his face with a coy expression before Charlotte had time to reply. Just as well. She felt a little bit annoyed with Sophia for being so bold. Also, Sophia would be sure to get the lead in the play, her uncle being the pianist and all.

Jock's hair was black, and his skin was dark, but his eyes were very light mauvish-blue, like fading lilacs, and he had a cleft chin. Charlotte was startled. He looked a lot like her father, she thought. And he acted like him, too. Gentlemanly, except when he got on his union high horse.

Mrs. Tweedsmuir clapped her hands and looked important. "All right now, everyone. When I was on the stage in England, we had some smashing hits, and I'm sure, with the proper effort, we can have a smashing hit right here in Extension. But first of all we must recruit more actors and actresses. And singers. Especially singers. *The Mikado* calls for versatility and self-discipline. Tell everyone you know that auditions will be held here on Tuesday."

Sophia twisted her hands in mock pleading and rolled her eyes. "I hope I get to be Yum Yum."

Charlotte couldn't keep an edge of resentment out of her voice. "Of course you will, if you want. Your Uncle Mario will see to that."

"No, not necessarily," Sophia said, stamping her foot with a little wiggle of her hips.

"Come on, Sophia, he's the best piano player in town, and this is a musical. You can be sure you'll get to be Tum Tum or Zum Zum or whatever the heck her name is, if you want to be." Charlotte guessed she'd get to be the boring ugly one, if anything. Maybe she wouldn't even join their silly play. She turned away and started to talk to a girl who sat beside her in the church choir. One thing about choir: it did teach people to sing half decently.

❦

Six days later, on January 14, there was a heavy snow-storm. The following afternoon the snow was still falling. It was so dark and dreary in the McEwan kitchen that Mabel lit the coal-oil lamp. Suddenly it sputtered and hissed.

"Danny McEwan, you quit playing with that lamp this very minute, or I'll skin you alive," his mother called out from the pantry.

"I didn't do anything," Danny said. "How come I always get in heck all the time..." But his words were lost in a thundering roar, and the house trembled on its foundations.

"Lord, preserve us! Not another mine accident. Please, God." Mabel grabbed Danny's hand, and they ran outside. People were racing toward the pithead, screaming, yelling questions.

"Another mining accident? How many men this time? Whose fathers and sons and brothers?"

But it wasn't the mine. The coal in a ship loaded with black powder had caught fire in Departure Bay. The captain ordered full speed out of the harbour, intending to get the crew off in the lifeboat, and then abandon ship himself when it was far enough away that it wouldn't be a danger to nearby residents. They lost the lifeboat in their frenzy, but they did manage to get to Protection Island. A young mother and her two children had run down to the beach to watch the blazing vessel approach, and the crew just managed to grab them and take cover when it exploded and burned to the water line. The one blessing was that nobody was killed.

Windows in the school and many of the houses in Nanaimo were broken, lots of people were cut by flying glass, and the pithead wharves at Protection Mine were ruined.

It was 7:30 by the time Charlotte finished the kitchen chores and left for rehearsal. It seemed as if every man, woman, and child in Extension was outside as she walked along the road, and they were all hopping mad. Angry gestures accompanied loud voices. "Bloody crime, that's what it is.... They've got no right to be making black powder and dynamite so close by.... They'll kill us all before they're done.... As if the bleeding mines aren't bad enough."

Casting for the play had already started by the time Charlotte arrived, and Sophia rushed to meet her. "I got

the part! Mrs. Tweedsmuir says I'm definitely the Yum
Yum type of person," she said breathlessly. She leaned
closer and whispered in Charlotte's ear. "Jock is going
to be Nanki-Poo. Oh, isn't it just too thrilling?"

"Mmm," Charlotte murmured.

"Charlotte, would you come here for a moment?"
Mrs. Tweedsmuir beckoned. "I've chosen you for a very
important role," she said, lifting Charlotte's hands in
her own. "You have a very nice alto voice, so you'll be
perfect to play the part of Katisha. You're the tallest.
Mind you, we'll have to pad you so you'll look fatter, and
you'll need to practise walking like you weigh a hundred
pounds more than you do." Mrs. Tweedsmuir babbled
on, but Charlotte had stopped listening.

So, she was going to be the big ugly one. She felt
like just not doing it. She had to admit that Sophia did
have the right colour of hair, even if it was too curly,
and the right kind of skin, even if her face was too fat—
and the right uncle.

And Jock Williamson was going to be Nanki-Poo. He
seemed so much like her dad, Charlotte thought. Even
her mother liked him, except she got nervous when he
talked about a union. But if Sophia had her way, he
wouldn't have time to spend on unions, or be friends
with her family anymore.

"Is something wrong, Charlotte?" Mrs. Tweedsmuir
asked, interrupting her thoughts.

"No, no. Nothing," Charlotte mumbled.

❦

Every afternoon, for two weeks, Charlotte rode the train
to Nanaimo one day, Ladysmith the next, and trudged

the streets looking for a job. Then she started to knock on the doors of every house in Extension, except in Chinatown and Japantown, asking if they had any ironing, baking, floor scrubbing, or anything at all that she might do to earn a little money.

But she had no luck, so she worked extra-hard at other things to keep her mind from dwelling on it.

Charlotte gathered up all the tins and jars of grease they had saved when rendering chunks of fat—which were sometimes free from the meat market or from a farmer—and the drippings from roasts, sausages, and chickens, and she boiled it all together in a kerosene can. She drained off the clear liquid, threw away the muddy dregs, added a tin of lye, boiled it all again, and poured it into an old roasting pan. When it hardened, it would keep them supplied with soap all winter—they just had to cut off a chunk when they needed it.

She dug for clams, repaired some loose and broken boards on the fence, and chopped kindling wood.

Sometimes she took the train to Ladysmith and borrowed a rowboat. She went fishing for salmon, brought it home, and then preserved it in quart sealers. The windows in the little house steamed up on those days by the time the jars had been boiled for five and a half hours in an enamel pot. She buried the fish innards, heads, and tails in the garden; deep enough, she hoped, to keep bears from smelling them and coming around.

THREE

One day Charlotte heard some news that made her heart beat faster and a surge of hope rise within her. The dynamite plant at Departure Bay was hiring, and they liked young girls to work for them, because their touch was more delicate. Charlotte was sure she could make her touch as delicate as the next girl, or Chinese man, who were also favoured for the same reason.

There were a couple of problems, to be sure. For one, there had been explosions, and folks said it was dangerous work—but so what? Nothing was perfect, and it couldn't be as dangerous as working in the mine. The other problem was that Departure Bay was a considerable distance from Extension, on the outskirts of Nanaimo. She would have to ride the train to the top of the Departure Bay hill and walk the rest of the way. If only they would hire her, she would figure out a way to get there, even if it meant finding a place to live nearby.

She had never seen the dynamite plant at close quarters, and she was surprised by how many buildings there were. Eight wooden structures of assorted shapes and sizes zigzagged down the hillside to the cliff at the ocean's edge. The lower six were connected by wooden sidewalks and a narrow-gauge railway track.

Mr. Tweedsmuir was interviewing hopeful candidates in front of the small office building. He wore a dark-grey-and-black-striped wool suit with a double-breasted jacket, a white shirt with a stiff wing collar, a black homburg hat with the brim snapped down in front, and lace-up shoes with shiny toe caps. Mr. Tweedsmuir was just about the most dashing figure of a man that Charlotte had ever seen.

He was half of a matched pair with Mrs. Tweedsmuir. She had been on the stage in England, and she was sure she could make *The Mikado* into a smash hit in Extension. They might even stage it at the Opera House in Nanaimo, she had said at the last rehearsal.

The dynamite plant had to be a pretty high-class place to work, Charlotte thought, if the manager could dress like that and had a wife who was a star.

Mr. Tweedsmuir smiled at her. "Experience, love?"

Charlotte looked at his shoes. "I beg your pardon?"

"Experience. What manner of work have you done before?"

"Well, sir, I...um...I've done housework, minded kids, baking, sewing, and..."

"Yes, yes, quite so. But I'm referring to proper employment. An avocation. Nursing, teaching, clerking, and so forth."

Charlotte shook her head and stared at his lapel. "No, sir."

"How old are you, love?"

She slipped her arm behind her back with her fingers crossed. "Sixteen."

"Education?"

"Yes, sir. I went to school." She was flooded with disappointment. He wouldn't hire her. Why should he? He had dozens of people to pick from—people who were smart, nicely dressed, and knew how to talk.

Suddenly her backbone stiffened with determination. She had to convince him she would be a better bet than any of the others. She lifted her chin and looked him in the eye.

"I had to quit in Grade Eight because my father got killed in the mine, but I did just fine in school. Really well, in fact. I took two grades in one year, and I was always head of the class." She had never bragged about herself before, and it felt strange, but nice, in a way. "And I won a medal for best student, and I could be a nurse soon as I'm old enough..." Oh-oh, she shouldn't have mentioned age.

"Let me see your hands."

Charlotte pulled off her gloves, stuffed them in her pocket, and held her hands out, palms down, for his inspection. Her hands were narrow, her fingers long, and her nails short. There were still a few dark patches where all her scrubbing hadn't succeeded in removing coal-dust stains, but she was glad she had taken time to push back the cuticles and use white pencil under her fingernail tips.

Mr. Tweedsmuir reached for her hands and turned them over, then he looked her up and down. "You'll do."

Charlotte swallowed. "I'll...do?"

"Yes, m'love. You'll do. Can you start Monday? The wage is one dollar and twenty-five cents a day."

"Yes, sir." She stared at her hands, still raised in front of her, as though she had never seen them before, then dropped them and pulled her gloves from her pocket.

He pointed. "See the foreman in that building down there. You can get signed up. But be careful. You can't go in without coveralls and the proper boots. Give a knock, and he'll come out and see to it. Good day." He watched while she pulled on her gloves, then offered his hand to shake.

"That building there," Charlotte learned later, was the packing and rolling house, but she caught only glimpses of long tables with people in white coveralls standing beside them when the foreman opened the door in response to her knock. He quickly dismissed her and told her they would do the paperwork on Monday morning. At 7:00 a.m. sharp.

Charlotte rode home on the train in a daze.

She had a job! Mr. Tweesdmuir had said she would do. A real job. Miss Charlotte Grace McEwan was now employed by Canadian Explosives Limited. Six days a week, 7:30 to 5:00. And the pay! She could hardly believe it. One dollar and twenty-five cents a day. It wouldn't even be hard work, not nearly as hard as washing clothes and scrubbing floors. She would be able to have a new dress, and Robbie wouldn't have to scramble for free coal. They could have chicken on Sundays, and Bea could have as many hair ribbons as she wanted. Next Christmas Danny would get the red wagon he had been longing for.

Charlotte would give some money to her mother every

payday, so she could quit worrying.

She might be late going to rehearsals, though. Maybe she should quit. If it took an hour to get each way like it had today, it would be touch and go.

But she had to remember to save some money, Charlotte thought. Just wait until Sophia found out. She would be bound to say something was wrong with it. Just sour grapes. In a year or so they could move to Victoria, or even back to Scotland, although her mother said times were harder there than here.

Her mother! How could she tell her where the job was? Maybe she could say it was at the post office or somewhere like that. The trouble was, somebody else would be sure to tell her mother the truth. But her mother couldn't stop her, Charlotte said to herself. She was determined to be the best dynamite packer they ever had. She'd just be careful, that was all. Maybe she'd even get to be a shift foreman, but probably not. Charlotte expected they gave those kinds of jobs to the men. She would tell her mother first thing in the morning.

The next day it seemed to take forever to get Beatrice off to school. She had been chosen to be on the drill team and she was excited.

"I get to wear blue bloomers, all puffy and pleated, like this," she said, flipping her hands around her thighs. "And a middy with a blue stripe on the bottom." She twirled around, and patted her mother's knee. "But don't worry, Mum. We don't have to pay for them."

The drill team would be marching in the Miners' Day Parade, and Beatrice hummed a marching tune and showed them how she could keep time to the music. "Pretend this is my wand," she said, waving a large spoon as she moved.

"That's very nice, Bea," her mother said. "Now off to school you go."

"You'll come and watch me, won't you, Mum, and Charlotte?" she said, standing with the front door open.

"Of course we'll come," her mother said.

Danny was playing with clothespins, picking them out of a cloth bag one at a time and piling them on a slab of wood. His "lobbing truck," he called it.

"Logging," his mother absentmindedly said.

"I know that," Danny said.

"Mother?" Charlotte asked.

"Hmm?" Mabel was sitting on a wooden kitchen chair, one her husband had made ten years before. Her elbows were on the table, and she had her chin in her hands and a cup of half-cold tea in front of her.

Charlotte tried to put just the right degree of excitement into her voice. "Mother, I've got a job. I'll be getting one dollar and twenty-five cents a day. You can stop taking in washing, and we can buy lots of food, and coal. We can *buy* our own coal, and—"

Mabel McEwan dropped her arms onto the table and stared at her daughter. She looked stern and suspicious. "What kind of job, Charlotte?"

"At CEL."

"The dynamite plant?"

"Yes. We can put some money by, and you can get a new suit for going to town, and maybe Bea can have piano lessons. You know how she can carry a tune. And—"

There was a dull clatter as Danny's "truck" collided with the woodbox and tipped over, sending clothespins spinning across the floor.

"Not making dynamite, Lottie? You're not making

dynamite. That's too dangerous. Not all the money in the world would convince me to let you do that."

"No, no. Not *making* it. Just taking orders and sending out bills in the office, Mum. Not making it." Charlotte almost convinced herself that the lie was true.

"Are you sure? How far away is the office from the plant?"

"Quite a ways. Remember the explosion a couple of years ago? The office didn't get touched."

"Seems to me I recall the windows got broken."

"Yes. Of course the windows got broken a bit, but now they're all changed to a different kind—sort of like French windows, so they'll fly open if need be."

"Pick those up, Daniel. A body could step on one of them and take a nasty fall." Mabel glanced over her shoulder. "Oh, Lottie, I don't know. I just don't know. You're a good reliable girl. I never could have managed without you. Are you sure it's perfectly safe? I couldn't withstand another one of my own being in an explosion."

"Perfectly safe, Mother. There haven't been many problems, only two, three, little blowups in ten years."

"Wait a minute now, Lottie. It seems to me that a few people have been killed in the two or three little blowups you're talking about." She was silent and still for several seconds, listening, concentrating, or thinking—whatever it was she did when she was like that. "Still, all in all, I daresay it would be a blessing to have steady money coming in. You're *sure* the office isn't close to any dynamite?"

"I'm sure, Mum."

"When do you start?"

"Monday."

"All right then. I'll go with you on Monday, just to see what it's all about."

"No, no. Not Monday. Later. Monday's the day they teach me how to do all the orders. I'll be nervous enough, but if you're there it would be kind of...you know, like I'm just a little kid. Lots of boys way younger than me work in the mines and that's a hundred times more dangerous than the office at the dynamite plant. Please, Mum, I'll be ever so careful. I promise," Charlotte said, lacing her fingers together.

Mabel sighed. "Seems like you've got your heart set on it, Lottie."

"I do, Mother, I do."

"All right, then. Try it out for a while, and we'll see. I'll talk to some of the neighbours, and see what they have to say."

Charlotte was anxious about what the neighbours might say, but at least she might have a chance to establish her reputation as a working person in the meantime.

"Thank you, Mum. I'll be fine. You'll see."

The village of Extension was looking more and more deserted. The company had built the houses and offered them to experienced miners at a reasonable rent as an inducement for them to leave their jobs and travel to Canada to work. Now the houses stood empty, as the company evicted striking miners from their homes. Families moved in with relatives, or built little shacks. It would be a hard winter. Old Number One was quiet. There was talk of strikebreakers coming, but Nanaimo's mines were still working. Folks were saying it was just a matter of time.

Big meetings attended by nearly two thousand miners

were held in Nanaimo, and those who wanted a union were trying hard to get their colleagues to join them.

Up until this time Chinese men hadn't been allowed to go down into the mines. They had worked above-ground, picking the rock out from the coal, loading, and hauling, and caring for the mules. Now there was talk that they were being threatened by the company to go back to work, or they would be returned to China. Going back to work made them scabs, and as the strike dragged on many of them were sent down to mine the coal.

Pro-union meetings were held once a week to keep spirits from flagging, and there were weekly dances to raise money for the cause. It was five cents apiece—the musicians played for nothing, the women took sand-wiches and cakes, and a good time was had by all.

The Knights of Pythias Hall looked and sounded a lot different for a dance than for *The Mikado* rehearsals. Paper streamers were hung on the walls; powdered wax was sprinkled on the floor; a pianist, a drummer, and a fiddler tuned up onstage; children chased each other over benches and around little knots of people in con-versation; and the smell of perfume, boiling coffee, mothballs, and perspiration mingled with the odour of kerosene given off by the lamps. Young girls slid and swirled their skirts on the dance floor to spread the wax.

The orchestra struck up a waltz. There was a tap on Charlotte's shoulder, and she turned.

"Come on, Charlotte, teach me to dance." It was Jock Williamson.

"I will," Sophia spoke up, turning on her brightest smile, but Jock offered his arm to Charlotte, and she accepted.

They had fun. Jock was definitely in need of dancing lessons. He had two left feet, as Charlotte had often heard her mother say about her father, and they laughed at his mistakes and kept starting over.

Sophia was pouting when Charlotte rejoined her.

"Why didn't you let me teach him?" she asked angrily. "You know perfectly well I said I was going to set my cap for him. Some friend you are!" She turned away with a flounce.

Although there was only two years' difference in their ages, Sophia and Charlotte were quite dissimilar in appearance and demeanour. Sophia had olive skin, black curly hair, dark brown eyes, and laughing, dimpled cheeks. She was "pleasingly plump," with a big bosom and a way of walking that made her hips sway. Although girls of seventeen weren't considered grown up, she had borrowed one of her mother's formal gowns with a raised waistline, lots of fringe, a wide cowl around the shoulders, and a large pink tulle rose in front.

Charlotte was skinny by comparison. Her straight light brown hair was plaited in two braids at the back of her head and held together with a blue satin ribbon. Her eyes were hazel and set deeply into the sockets, which gave her a waifish, hungry look. Her face was narrow, and she had her pretty mother's full-lipped mouth, only on Charlotte it looked more stern and determined. She wore the same dress she had worn to every party for the past year: an ankle-length blue gingham with a ruffle around the neckline and sleeves.

Everybody stopped moving and looked toward the stage as Jock's voice, amplified by a megaphone, echoed around the room. "Ladies and gentlemen, may I have your attention please? Will all the miners step outside?

There's a spot of trouble at the pithead, and we need to do a little planning."

"What? Oh, my goodness. I'm glad my father's not on shift," Sophia said, looking relieved at the thought. "My father's just about the only one allowed in the mines now, being a fire boss. But he's not working tonight."

The miners moved fast, and within five minutes the hall was empty of all but women, children, and old men.

"Robbie, where are you going?" Charlotte demanded.

"Nowhere. Just outside for a minute." Robbie was with two other boys of about the same age, and they were heading for the door.

"You better stay out of trouble. That's none of your business."

FOUR

The air was still and cold, and men's angry voices could be heard in the distance as Charlotte and Sophia walked home with a group of other girls, supervised by the young married woman who was their chaperone.

"Too bad he didn't have time to ask me to dance," Sophia said.

Charlotte stopped and looked around. "Who? I wonder where Robbie's at."

"Jock Williamson, of course, you ninny. Too bad he didn't get a chance. I know he would have asked me for the supper waltz."

"Probably," Charlotte said, distracted. "Robbie?" she called out.

Twenty minutes later Charlotte's mother asked, "Why

didn't you bring him home with you? I don't like him out this late, with all the talk of strikebreakers and hiring extra police. Some of the places that are boarded up have been broken into and folks' belongings taken. I don't like it at all."

"I couldn't stop him, Mother. I tried. He's bound to turn up soon."

Robbie did turn up eventually, with his Sunday-best pants ripped and a bloody nose.

"Just fell, is all, Ma. Me 'n Jim 'n Angus, we were hiding behind some stumps, 'cause the police were heading up to the mine. And then we heard a shot, so we beat it outta there as fast as we could go. And I fell, and..." Robbie grinned at her. "Sorry, I ripped my pants. You can fix 'em, can't you?"

"I suppose," his mother said with a sigh. "Robert James McEwan, you'll be the death of me yet."

🛒

Charlotte got up at five o'clock on Monday morning, and she was nervous. What if she couldn't learn to make dynamite properly? Exactly what did making dynamite mean, anyway? How did they do it? What if she made mistakes or couldn't do it fast enough? She tried to act confident, as if going to work was just an everyday occurrence during the twenty-minute walk and the half-hour train ride to Departure Bay.

She knocked on the door of the packing and rolling house. The door was opened by the foreman, who held a pair of white coveralls.

"Rule number one is no pockets," he said. "Might have matches. No pockets, no matches. Understand?"

"Yes, sir."

"Put this on." He handed her the white coveralls. "Change in the wash house, second building up," he said, pointing with his thumb. "Another thing, everybody has to wear these boots." He gestured to his feet. "Made without nails. Nails can cause sparks, and then look out! This place could blow sky-high. Poof!" He sounded as matter-of-fact as if he were talking about the weather, while at the same time he raised his hands in an explosionlike gesture. "No metal allowed. The shovels are made of wood. All the tools are made out of paper. Understand?"

"Yes, sir. Um, where do you get the boots, sir?"

"Right there." He indicated a shed just outside the door.

Two men were carefully manoeuvring a four-wheeled wooden cart with a wooden handle along the railway track as Charlotte returned to the packing and rolling house. They stopped at the door and began to unload large containers. Was there dynamite in them? She would soon find out.

The foreman led Charlotte, wearing her coveralls and boots, to a long table. "This is Runty. He'll teach you the ropes."

Runty was small and cross-eyed, and his hair was messy. He greeted Charlotte with a grin. "You'll get headaches. Nitro does it. Don't touch your forehead. You're lucky you're a girl."

"Why?"

"Girls get over it faster."

"You mean everybody gets headaches?"

Runty nodded. "At first they do. Don't worry. You'll do fine."

A Chinese man was standing on the other side of Charlotte. He kept his head down and didn't speak to her or even glance her way, so she touched his shoulder and smiled. "I'm Charlotte."

He pointed to her. "Aw Lot." Then he put his hand on his chest, nodded, and said, "Aw Lee."

"Is this the dynamite then?" Charlotte asked as she watched Runty and Aw Lee roll a brown substance into eight-inch-long cylindrical sticks. It certainly didn't look dangerous.

"That's what she is." Runty said. "Called gelignite. Not as dangerous as black powder. Not to use, that is. Dangerous to mix, though."

"So, where do they mix it?"

"Top of the hill. In the nitrator."

"What's it made out of?"

"Nitroglycerin and kieselguhr."

"Kiesel-what?"

"Kieselguhr. A sort of fine dirt. Mixes with the nitro. It makes it solid so it can be rolled. Like cigars. See?"

Aw Lee nodded, agreeing with Runty, and pretended to smoke one.

Charlotte was nervous and clumsy at first, but as she watched Runty and Aw Lee handle the brown mixture, rolling it out just so, and then wrapping the cylinders in brown paper and placing them in a wooden packing crate, she gained confidence. By the end of the day, she was finishing one stick for every two of theirs.

"I wish I could get faster," she said.

Runty shook his head. "Not to worry. You're catching on mighty quick."

Aw Lee nodded. "Plenny quick."

Charlotte did get bad headaches, but by Saturday,

they had stopped. It seemed as though all she did for six days was ride the train to work, stand all day rolling and wrapping sticks of dynamite while pretending they were cigars, ride the train home, get washed, have supper, go to bed, and get up the next morning to go to work again. Sunday meant church, dinner at noon, and sometimes a walk or a visit to the cemetery.

One Sunday, when Charlotte got home from watching Bea's drill practice, her mother was standing on the front porch with her hands on her hips. Her cheeks were flushed and her eyes were blazing.

"All right, Charlotte Grace McEwan. Get in here this minute and tell me exactly what's going on!"

Charlotte gulped. "What do you mean, what's going on?"

"Don't play the innocent with me, my girl. Out with it before I...I." Mabel made an angry gesture with her hand. "It's a pretty sorry day when I have to find out from the neighbours what my own daughter is up to."

"You mean about my job?" Charlotte's palms were sweating, and she rubbed her hands nervously.

"That's exactly what I mean. Sit down!" Mabel yanked a chair toward the table, thumped herself down on it, and pointed to the bench.

Charlotte's hands shook as she pulled out the bench and sat. "Come on, Mum. It's not like you think. I did start out in the office and I had a chance to work in the plant, but— No, that's not true. I started in the plant. But it really isn't dangerous. In fact, it's safe, as safe as can be, and—"

Mabel had her arms on the table and her hands clasped tightly together. "Charlotte, look at me."

Charlotte reached for her mother's hands. "It's because

of the money, Mum. Don't you see? I want us to get out of this place. All of us." She gazed into her mother's brown eyes through a blur of tears.

"I do, Lottie. I do understand." Mabel took Charlotte's hand in both of her own. "I know you're only trying to help. But I don't want anything to happen to you." Her lower lip trembled, and tears pooled in the corners of her eyes.

Charlotte leaned toward her mother, her voice thick with tears. "It's okay, Mum. Mr. Tweedsmuir says he'll teach me bookkeeping and other office duties when an opportunity arises, as he calls it. So you see, I'll probably be working in the office pretty soon."

"The hardest thing is, you didn't tell me the truth."

"But you wouldn't let me work there if I did."

"No. I surely would not." Mabel took a handkerchief from her apron pocket and blew her nose, then sat absolutely still for several seconds while Charlotte prayed that she wouldn't have to quit the job. "We'll let bygones be bygones for now," her mother said finally. "That doesn't mean I agree with it, mind. We need a cup of tea." She stood, patted Charlotte's shoulder, and reached for the teapot.

Charlotte's anxiety was mixed with relief. Keeping a secret from her mother had been the hardest thing she could ever remember doing. She felt as though she had been living under a cloud and it had suddenly lifted. Not that her mother was happy, far from it, but at least she didn't have to pretend she wasn't working with dynamite anymore.

"This is our only chance to get out of here, as far as I can see," she said to her mother's back. "I just want to get enough money saved, but it's harder than I thought.

We have only twenty-seven dollars in the bank so far. I shouldn't have bought the material for a new dress."

Mabel turned and brandished the teapot in the air to emphasize her words. "You are indeed going to have a new dress, Lottie. That's the least you deserve. And there's enough material left over for a pinafore for Bea. She's counting on it."

"I'm going to save my new dress for Dominion Day. July 1 is on a Tuesday. A holiday in the middle of the week—I can hardly wait. The picnic on Newcastle Island is just about my favourite thing. One thing I feel sorry about, though." With her forefinger, Charlotte traced the floral design on the oilcloth that covered the table. "Besides not telling the truth, I mean."

Mabel set a plate of oatmeal cookies and a cup of tea in front of Charlotte. "And what might that be?"

"Mr. Tweedsmuir asked me to go in to work on any holidays that come up. He said I'd get paid extra, and it would be a good chance for me to learn the office routine with nobody else around."

Mabel's head jerked up, and she stared at her daughter. "I hope you didn't go along with it."

"I said I couldn't. But maybe I should tell him I can, so I can get an office job faster."

Mabel shook her head. "No. I don't think that would be quite proper. Not without a chaperone."

"But Mr. Tweedsmuir is married, Mum."

"Yes, I've heard his wife is very nice."

"And he's nice, too. He's just trying to help me get ahead."

While they had their tea they talked about the strike.

"It's looking bad," Mabel said. "They've got twenty-one special policemen in Extension now, just to take the new miners to work. They don't even live in the empty houses, like you'd think they would. They live up near the mine. Bullpens is what they call the place they stay."

"I think Nanaimo's going to join in the strike," Charlotte said, "and then look out. Jock hates the scabs. He says he'd rather starve than be a scab. He says it would stay with you all your life. They'd keep calling you scabbie and spit at you, and if you had kids, they'd call your kids names, too. Some of the men coming in as strike-breakers don't know the real truth about things until they get here. Too bad for them. Jock says things will get worse before they get better, but I don't think they can get much worse than they are, do you?" She looked at her mother anxiously.

Mabel shrugged. "I don't know. We have worries enough of our own, Lottie. Nobody under fourteen is allowed out after eight, but I know Robert sneaks out. Did you hear about the three boys, only twelve they were, put in jail for four hours for stealing chickens? And one was fined ten dollars for torturing a cow! A poor helpless creature like that."

"But Robbie would never harm an animal, Mum, you know that. And he wouldn't steal, either. I'd bet my life on it."

"You're right. He says he's going to get a job at the pithead as soon as the strike's over, getting the coal cars together to go back down, or filling powder cans for the miners. I wish he would get rid of that notion. He's pretty young, but they do hire thirteen-year-olds sometimes if they fib about their age." She stirred her tea absent-mindedly.

"If he does, then the next thing you know he'll be down in the tunnel, and I don't want that any more than you do," Charlotte said. "Maybe I should have said I would go into the office like Mr. Tweedsmuir wants, to learn faster and be sure of the money."

"I don't think so, Lottie. You need a treat now and then."

"I don't care so much about Miners' Day, except that I told Bea I would go, but I do want to go to the picnic, what with my new dress and all. People will think I'm getting up in the world." Charlotte paused. "Maybe Robbie would listen to a man more than to us. Why don't you ask Jock to talk to him? He likes Jock."

"Yes, he does. But Jock would fill his head with union talk, and Robert might get involved and earn himself a bad reputation. Nobody would ever give him a chance at a decent job then. Oh, dear." Mabel brushed her hair back from her forehead with her hand and stared into her teacup. "What would I do without you, Charlotte?"

She raised her eyes, and her face looked so haggard and tired that Charlotte wanted to cry. "Maybe we can get out of here before it gets much worse," Charlotte said. "I'm going to try harder to save money. No more new clothes, and Bea is going to have to stop the piano. It seems a waste, anyway, when she has to go to her teacher's house to practise and can only do it twice a week for half an hour."

Mabel rose and looked out the window. "Well, I'll be. Looks to me like the curly lilies are in bloom."

Charlotte rushed to her mother's side. "They are. I'll pick some for you, Mum."

"Not too many, mind. Your father would only pick a few. He said he was pretty sure that once you picked them they wouldn't come back the next year."

"I know," Charlotte agreed as she ran out of the

house toward the field.

More than any other flower, curly lilies reminded Charlotte of her father. He had picked wildflowers for his wife almost every Sunday. All of them were nice in their own special way, but the memory of his rough coal-mining hands holding delicate curly lilies always made her smile.

She was smiling now as she picked the flowers and remembered other things about those days. The way he polished everybody's shoes on Sunday morning before church, how he always managed to find a sweetpea, a daisy, or a blossom of some kind to wear in his button-hole, and the sound of his hymn-singing voice in her ears. She stood among the lilies and thought about how different life would be if he were still alive. And Janet, too.

It would be nice to have a twelve-year-old sister to talk to. What would she look like now? She had been full of fun before she got sick—always laughing and joking. Charlotte wished there could be more flower-picking and singing and joking in her family now, but there didn't seem to be much to sing and joke about these days.

FIVE

The following Sunday afternoon Charlotte went for a walk with Sophia. Her friend wore a grown-up version of a child's middy dress. The ankle-length garment was made of grey silk crepe and was pleated down the front of the skirt, with eight large buttons between the waist and hip holding the two pleats in place. The slightly gathered bodice was cinched with a patent-leather belt, and a wide sailor-style collar with a chiffon scarf and a brooch just showing under the V at the front completed the innocent yet sophisticated look. The sleeves were long and narrow. A large pink satin bow at the back of her head framed her loosely rolled hair.

Charlotte wore a denim skirt and a hand-knit blue sweater. Her braids were tied together at the back of her head with a piece of knitting wool.

This time Charlotte had vowed she wouldn't let Sophia make her feel like an ugly duckling. After all, she had a job and Sophia didn't. She would tell her friend only the good things about her job.

"I haven't seen you in ages," Sophia said. "How come you quit coming to rehearsals?"

"I'm too tired when I finish supper and washing up—and I have to get up by five."

"Gracious me. I could never get up at that unearthly hour. However in the world do you do it?"

"I have to if I want to keep my job," Charlotte replied, emphasizing the word *job*.

"I suppose," Sophia sniffed. "Poor you."

"It's not so bad. The money's good."

"Mmm. I suppose. I might be getting a job at the hospital, learning to be a nurse."

"Oh, I hope you do," Charlotte said, secretly hoping nurses didn't get paid as much as dynamite packers.

"Tell me about *your* job," Sophia said. "What's it like?"

"The people at work are nice. The man who stands beside me is called Runty. He's okay—kind of little and funny-looking and he's friendly as can be. A Chinese man works on the other side. He's nice, too. He calls me Aw Lot and his name is Aw Lee, or something like that, so the others call us Lot and Lee. He's a good worker, and he warns me by the look on his face and the way he moves his hands to be ever so careful. Aw Lee really likes little kids, smiles at them, and gives them ginger candy when we pass them on the way home. It's too bad he can't have a wife and some kids of his own."

"How come?" Sophia asked.

"None of the Chinese men can have wives here. You hardly ever see any Chinese women, do you?"

"No, but I guess the men like living all crammed together like that. They're different from us, you know," said Sophia with a lift of her chin.

"Sophia, they don't like it," Charlotte said crossly. "They want wives and kids just like everybody else, but they can't afford it."

"Why can't they? They have jobs."

Charlotte felt as if she was explaining something patiently to Danny. "Because it costs fifty dollars each for them to come here in the first place, which they have to pay back to the company. I don't know about the dynamite plant, but I do know that the Chinese men who work at the mines only get paid half as much as the other men."

"Too bad for them," Sophia said.

Charlotte stopped walking and put her hands on her hips. "It is too bad," she said angrily.

Sophia raised her hands at shoulder level and grimaced. "All right, don't get your shirt in a knot. Go ahead and feel sorry for them if you want. It's up to you."

"Oh, I give up," Charlotte muttered.

Sophia changed the subject. "But what do you *do* all day long at work?"

Charlotte shrugged. "Oh, I roll and wrap and pack. Of course, it's not all beer and skittles, as Jock says, but—"

The mention of Jock's name caused Sophia to frown, and she grabbed Charlotte's arm. "When did you see him?"

"He sometimes comes over at night, after the union meetings, to see if he can help—"

Sophia interrupted again. "Well, I don't understand it. I *never* get a chance to talk to him. He comes to rehearsals, but he rushes in at the last minute and leaves early. Why don't I come over and visit you at night, too?"

"Aw, Sophie, I'm too tired to talk to anybody after supper."

"How come you're not too tired to talk to Jock then?"

"I don't. I go to bed. He talks to my mother and Robbie."

Sophia stopped abruptly. "Okay, for you," she said angrily. "Some friend you are. You know perfectly well I want him for my beau, and you won't even stay up a little later to help me out."

Charlotte sighed. "Don't be mad, Sophia. You can come over."

"Thanks, Char. I knew you were a real friend." She put her arm around Charlotte's waist and fell into step beside her.

"Oh, Sophia, there's something I want to ask you. Do you remember a girl called Sybil? She had my job before me."

"I didn't really know her, but I know who you mean."

"Do you know why she quit?"

Sophia shook her head. "She left town, that's all I know. Went to stay with her aunt or somebody. What time does Jock usually come around?"

"Different times. Sometimes I'm already in bed when he comes, but it's usually around nine."

"Good. I'll see you then." Sophia waved two fingers at Charlotte and turned toward home.

♦

On Monday morning Charlotte was rolling dynamite sticks carefully with her delicate touch the way Runty and Aw Lee had taught her.

"Here comes old Tweedy," Runty said, leaning sideways.

Charlotte glanced up. "You're right, Runty. Keep busy!"

"Wonder what's up."

Charlotte shrugged and concentrated on her hands.

Mr. Tweedsmuir's step slowed, and he stopped behind Charlotte. She kept her head down and her eyes on her work.

"Good morning, my dear," he said.

"Good morning, sir."

"Mornin', Mr. Tweedsmuir," Runty said.

"Charlotte, I, ah...remember our little conversation? About you coming into the office once in while to learn the ropes, so to speak?"

Charlotte nodded, and Runty sniffed.

"Perhaps, my dear, you'd like to come by for a little initiation after work today?"

"Sorry, sir. I wouldn't, I mean I couldn't...wouldn't get home in time if I stay. My mother would worry."

"Of course she would." He lowered his voice. "How extremely thoughtless of me. I know what we'll do. You quit a little early, say, around four-thirty, then you come to the office. Just tell the others you have a headache and need an aspirin."

Charlotte swallowed. "All right, sir."

She should be happy. At last she had a chance to learn a better job. It would be a big help to know how to do bookkeeping when, and if, they ever did move to a city. So why was she worried? Anxiety, that was it. Just anxiety about whether or not she could live up to his expectations and learn the things he was willing to teach her.

But when she was actually standing in his office he didn't seem in a hurry to teach her anything.

"Here, m'love, sit down. Would you care for a little

drop of something?"

Charlotte wasn't sure what he meant. "Pardon?"

He laughed and winked. "A dram. A wee *doch-an-doris*, as you Scotch like to call it."

She didn't know what to say. "I—"

"Of course, my dear. Don't look so worried. I was just pulling your leg. And a very pretty leg I'm sure it is, too, under those coveralls. Don't pay any notice. I was just teasing. Come on now, don't be shy. You like your job here, don't you?"

Charlotte's heart lurched. Was he going to tell her she was being let go? "Oh, yes, sir, very much."

"There could be better things in store for you. You're quick and pretty, as well. Yes, indeed, there could be a bright future waiting for you."

Charlotte really looked at him for the first time. He reminded her of a picture she had seen in a book long ago. His thin-lipped smile and his eyes half-hidden behind reflections on his gold-rimmed glasses stirred a memory— her grandmother's hands, turning pages, pointing.

"And look, lassie, here's a picture of..." But Charlotte couldn't bring the name to mind.

"Yes, sir" was all she could think to say.

"I've decided to take a personal interest in you, m'love. If you keep up the good work, cooperate just the way you have been doing, by this time next year you could be working steadily here in the office. Would you like that?"

"I don't know, sir."

"You don't have to call me sir." He leaned closer, put his hand on her arm, and gave it a little squeeze. Charlotte thought she could smell whiskey on his breath, but it might have been shaving cream or hair oil.

She pulled her arm away, looked at the floor, and entwined her hands.

"It's all right, m'love. No need to be upset now. We'll talk about it another day, once you've got yourself used to the idea. All right?"

Charlotte nodded and rose to leave.

"Allow me." He opened the door with a flourish and bowed her out.

By the end of June, all the miners were on strike except the scabs. Jock said the company was bringing in more strikebreakers from Scotland and the United States, and that there was real trouble brewing. One evening he had tea with Charlotte's mother.

"The miners have to win, to get a union, because the bosses don't care a whit for the workers," he said. "The company can tell a man to get out if they don't like the colour of his shirt, and the man has no comeback. And you have to produce, or they won't keep you. You're allowed fifty pounds of rock in a coal car. If they find fifty-one, you lose the whole car—you don't get paid for any of it. And if they send you to see the superintendant, he can decide whether to tell you to do better, or tell you to pick up your tools and go. Even if a man is a good worker, if they don't happen to like him they can fire him, and he can't do anything about it." Jock pounded the table with his fist.

Mabel folded her hands on her lap. "It surely is bad. Strange, Geordie didn't say more about that."

"I guess he didn't want to worry you," Jock said soothingly.

With more and more boarded-up empty houses, Nanaimo was beginning to look like Extension. The strikers were being evicted. At least the weather was warmer, so some could stay in tents. The women were behind the men, it seemed.

There were policemen everywhere. They had to go with the strikebreakers to work, or the miners wouldn't let them through. The special police didn't wear uniforms and weren't trained, and they were soon hated by everybody. They stole things, and they strutted along and jostled people out of their way, forcing them off the road.

Jock was one of the main union leaders, and people said he did a lot of the talking at the meetings. Charlotte thought he was pretty good at convincing other people to see things his way. He had almost convinced her that being a miner was a good, honest way to earn a living, but the debits outweighed the credits in Charlotte's books. She had learned about debits and credits from Mr. Tweedsmuir. She had been going in once a week at noon and was allowed to take a half hour extra while he showed her a few things about bookkeeping. She just wished he wouldn't stand so close.

One day, as Charlotte was leaving work, the watchman beckoned her. "Watch your step, lass. The one who was here before ye got the short end of it, the poor wee thing."

"What do you mean, Mr. Sykes?" she asked.

He looked alarmed. "I spoke out of turn. It's as much as my job's worth to be telling things that are none of my business. Forget I ever said a thing, will ye, lassie?"

Charlotte wondered if he meant Sybil. She wanted very badly to find out more about her. Why did she leave town so suddenly? But who could she ask? Mr. Tweedsmuir? He might know.

🔔

Charlotte was just dropping off to sleep one night when she heard somebody crying.

Mabel McEwan had an arm around Sophia's shoulder and was pulling her into the house as Charlotte ran down the stairs. "Come in, come in, girl. Whatever's the matter?"

Sophia was sobbing, her shoulders heaving, and her face was red and wet with tears. "My father. A bunch of men came and...and..."

"Poor child. Come and sit down." Mabel led the hysterical young woman to a chair, pushed her into it, and handed her a clean handkerchief.

"What's wrong?" Bea was standing on the stairs, rubbing her eyes with one hand and twisting the hem of her nightgown with the other.

"It's all right, Bea. Don't you worry." Her mother lifted her down the last few steps and set her on the bench beside the table. "Here. You can look at my knitting book. See if you can find a sweater you might fancy." She turned her attention back to Sophia. "And then what happened?"

Sophia's voice came out in small, hiccuping gasps. "They, they, yelled and called him names."

Finally the whole story was told.

A group of miners had come around yelling about "getting that bloody turncoat scab." They had banged on the walls and demanded that Luigi Carpelli come out and face the music.

"My father is a fire boss. He has to go in during the

strike. But they said now that scabs are working, he's a scab, too, if he keeps going to work."

"Where is your father now?"

"I don't know. Hiding out in the bush, I guess. But those men say they won't leave until he shows himself." Sophia buried her face in her hands and burst into a fresh bout of tears. "And my mother and my sisters are still in the house. And—"

"Come on," Charlotte said. "We'll get Jock to go and talk to them."

"No. I'm afraid. We'd better not go. Just tell the police or somebody."

"We're going. At least I am, if Jock will go with us. He can talk some sense into them." Charlotte grabbed her cape and pulled on her shoes.

Jock did talk sense to the men. "There's nobody inside but a woman and three girls, and they don't deserve this kind of treatment," he told the crowd. "How would you like it if people terrorized your womenfolk when you were away from home? Anyway, you all know Luigi Carpelli has to go down the mines, being a fire boss. It's necessary. A lot of you wouldn't be here today if it weren't for the fire bosses keeping an eye on things."

"That may be the truth of it, Williamson!" one irate striker shouted. "But now they got scabs working the mine, and that argument don't hold water no more."

"Listen, lads. I give you my word of honour that I'll talk to Luigi myself. He's a reasonable man. Anybody who knows him knows that. I'll talk to him, and I'll do my best to get him to see the union point of view. So, all of you just go home now. I'll talk to him as soon as he comes back, then I'll let you know what he says."

"Sure, Jock," one of the disgruntled men said. "All

right, if you say. But you better have the right answer pretty quick, or we'll be back for the scabbie."

The crowd left and marched up the road singing loudly.

SIX

Charlotte's life became more and more worrisome as the summer wore on. There was the strike, her mother worried about Robbie getting too big for his britches, and she worried about her mother. But the worst worry of all was about her job. She must not lose it!

Mr. Tweedsmuir kept coaxing her to go into the office on July 1 to have a good long lesson on book-keeping. When she told him about the picnic, he said, "The better the day, the better the deed," and that it would be a good time because everybody else would be over at Newcastle Island and they wouldn't be disturbed. He was very friendly, put his arm around her, and gave her a kiss on the cheek when she left. She didn't like the kiss because of his moustache, but for other reasons, too. Still, he was trying to help her. He said the plant might be closed soon, but bookkeeping jobs were easy to get. Some days, however, he didn't show her much. They just had a "friendly chat," as he called it, about her family, money, and living "nice" and not in a miner's cottage.

Mr. Carpelli turned out to be fine. He stayed away from home for a couple of days, which worried Mrs. Carpelli and the girls half to death. But he was just scratched up a bit and had sprained his wrist while being out in the bush. When he went into the pit again, it was if he were going to work as usual, but he was only there to pick up his belongings. He said he'd join the union, too, and Jock said that when the other men heard that, they all cheered and threw their hats in the air.

Sophia had lost her Yum Yum part in the play because of it, but now she was back in, and Charlotte was glad.

Charlotte tried asking Mr. Sykes more about Sybil, but he made her promise not to mention what he had already said. She promised. He was a nice man, but why did he tell her to watch her step? Watch her step around what? The dynamite?

❦

The new dress fitted just fine, and Charlotte felt like a real lady dressed up in it. Bea looked as cute as a button in her new pinafore, too.

Charlotte was still worried when picnic day arrived. She felt as if she were doing something wrong—playing hooky, giggling in church, or tattling on her brother. She should be going to the plant as Mr. Tweedsmuir had wanted. How could she expect to get ahead in the world if she didn't keep her nose to the grindstone?

By the time she had helped Bea and Danny have a bath in the tub in the middle of the kitchen floor, then had one herself and washed her hair, she began to feel better. She pulled her hair back loosely and fastened it with a wide satin bow at the back of her head and slipped the dress on over a brand-new petticoat. The petticoat was a surprise. Her mother had made it without her even knowing, and it was perfect, made of fine mercerized cotton instead of flour sacks. She felt like Cinderella, her work coveralls transformed into the most beautiful dress she could imagine. It was called a lingerie dress and was the very latest fashion. It was made of white cotton muslin with both the bodice and dirndl skirt gathered into a three-inch-wide waistband. Panels of fine embroidered eyelet curved around the top of the bodice just above the bustline, down the elbow-length sleeves, and around the hemline, which fell slightly above the ankle. It made her feel very grown-up with its narrow skirt and nipped-in waist. Not that she needed waist-nipping; her figure was slim and her legs were long, for a girl. Jock often teased her about that, calling her a "bonnie long drink of water."

It seemed a treat beyond compare—the new dress, the picnic, and the whole family going out together somewhere besides church or the cemetery. She felt as though she could be a lady for the rest of her life instead of turning back into a dynamite maker when the party was over.

Charlotte helped her mother carry the laundry basket packed with everything they would need, including enough food to last the day, even enough for Jock. Her mother had asked him when he brought over a loaf of store-bought bread and two frying chickens.

The tugboat *We Two* was anchored in the harbour, waiting to tow the old scow that usually carried miners to work across the narrow channel to the Protection Mine. The scow hadn't been used lately because of the strike, but the miners and their wives had managed to raise enough money to hire it for the day.

The McEwans inched down the gangplank sideways. Danny was in the lead, pulling at Charlotte's hand and trying to hurry them. Charlotte's other hand grasped the basket. Both of her mother's hands were occupied, between the basket and hanging on to Bea. A familiar Scottish brogue called from behind.

"Hold on a tick. Let me carry that."

The procession stopped, but it took some manoeuvring to transfer children's hands and basket handles while on the swaying gangplank. Finally Jock and Charlotte were carrying the basket between them, Mabel had one child on each side, and reaching hands helped them safely aboard the scow where they were surrounded by other laughing, chattering picnickers.

Jock looked at Charlotte when they were aboard. "You look pretty as a picture, lass." He sounded so much like her father that Charlotte pinched herself to make sure she wasn't dreaming.

Voices called out. "Jock, we need to talk to you. Come over here."

"Jock, old man, see you for a second?"

"Oh, all right." He moved to join a small knot of men who were huddled together.

The sun was shining, and Newcastle Island looked like a picture postcard as they approached: the sandy beaches; the green grassy knoll at the landing site; the tall fir trees; the multicoloured smaller bushes and shrubs; and the light-coloured summer clothing of the people who had already arrived made it look unreal.

Alice in Wonderland, that was what she felt like, Charlotte thought as they climbed the gangplank and walked up the sloping path to the grassy area. Something magical could happen here. Jock was back, helping to carry the basket, and Charlotte walked proudly, the soft petticoat brushing her white stockings making her feel almost naked after the heavy feel of her cotton drill coveralls. For once she was glad her hair wasn't curly. It felt like heavy silk as it swayed and brushed her shoulders when she moved.

Robbie had arrived already, and he came running to meet them, stopping with a skid to stare at Charlotte. "Hey, Lottie, you look different. What'd ya do to yourself? Here, I'll take that." He took the basket handle and started to talk "man talk" to Jock.

Bea and Danny had run ahead, so Charlotte dropped back to keep her mother company.

"You really do look grand in that dress, Lottie. A treat for the eyes," Mabel said.

"You did an extra-special good job, Mum. I love it." Charlotte stepped off the path, skipped a few steps, and whirled around with her arms held out at her sides. She felt like the belle of the picnic—for about twelve minutes, while they found a good spot under a big tree, spread their blankets, and talked about what they should do first. Then Sophia arrived, looking like the princess of the picnic.

Sophia wore a lingerie dress, too, but hers was pale blue with a blue satin sash at the waist. Its embroidered panels were much wider than those on Charlotte's dress.

Her large hat, woven of white straw, had blue fabric flowers around the brim, and she carried a blue parasol. She looked smashing.

"Hello, Jock." She offered her hand to shake and smiled up into his face, dimples dimpling, eyes sparkling. "Good morning, Mrs. McEwan. Hello, Charlotte. Would you like to take a walk to Kanaka Bay?" She addressed the question directly to Jock.

Jock turned and looked at them. "Charlotte? Mrs. McEwan? Would you care to go?"

Mabel leaned back against a tree trunk and pulled some knitting from the basket. "No, thank you. I'll just stay here and keep an eye on the children. Thank you just the same, Jock."

Jock, Sophia, and Charlotte had walked no more than two hundred yards when Jock was called again and asked to join a group of men who were lounging under a maple tree smoking cigarettes. One man was holding a notepad and a stub of a pencil, which he licked before using.

"After a bit. Just taking a walk," Jock told the men.

"Hey, look at that wouldja?" one miner said. "Williamson's got himself two beauties. Share the wealth, Jock. Don't be greedy, man."

The men all turned to stare at Charlotte and Sophia. Charlotte felt flustered. No one had ever called her a beauty before, and she had to admit the words made her feel pretty grown-up. She just wished she didn't feel seminaked, as if they could see right through her dress and petticoat. Some of those men were married, but just the same...

"We need you, Jock," another miner said. "Remember what we were talkin' about? This is sure-fire urgent now.

We've only got until tomorrow..."

"Shut up, Boyce! Keep your lip buttoned!" several miners shouted, while the other men looked around anxiously and spoke in low voices.

"I'll see you when you come back this way," Jock said to the girls.

"Sure," Sophia replied. "Why don't we sing songs from the play at the entertainment after?"

But Jock didn't answer. Instead, he settled himself on the grass with the other miners, and the murmur of their voices followed the girls along the cinder path.

Men played horseshoe pitch, tug-of-war, and football, while the kids played catch, hide-and-seek, Mumblety-peg, and duck on a rock. They took off their shoes and stockings and waded in the warm, shallow water between Newcastle and Protection Islands. Women sat together on blankets and laughed and talked, sharing recipes and quilting patterns and talking about the past times in the Old Country.

Most of the miners and their wives were Scottish and English, but there were also Italians, Slavs, and Finns. They were learning English, but when they were together they mostly spoke their own languages.

Charlotte and Sophia were joined by three other young women, and young unmarried men called out joking remarks to them, asking if they could come along, buy them a lemonade, or take them for a row. "I've got the cutest little dinghy you've ever seen," one said. "How about it?"

Charlotte lifted her head in a huff and walked on, but the others stopped to exchange laughing remarks and "give them back a taste of their own medicine," as Sophia later put it.

No sooner did Jock come back to the McEwans' blanket to eat than he was needed as pitcher in the baseball game. Shorty McPhee was calling him.

"I haven't finished eating yet," Jock said, waving a drumstick and shaking his head.

"All right. Ten minutes. We'd like to get the game started."

Sophia wanted to watch the baseball game and cheer for Jock, but Charlotte got bored after the first twenty minutes.

"I'm going for a walk," she announced.

Over the hill, away from the crowd, it was quiet. The path was dappled with sunshine, birds sang, leaves rustled, and a woodsy scent filled the air. Charlotte had almost forgotten how sweet and clean the outdoors could smell.

A small black-capped bird ran down a tree trunk, stopping now and then to peck. A squirrel darted across the path, stood on its hind legs to look at her, chattered something, then scampered off.

The lake was deep blue, reflecting trees and reeds. Five ducks swam by noiselessly, leaving gently widening wakes behind them. Charlotte knelt beside an old log to look for the lady's slippers she knew grew there, but they seemed to be finished for the year. She did find violets, both yellow and purple, some ripe huckleberries, two late-blooming trilliums, and a creamy gold mushroom that looked delicious but was probably poisonous. She crouched lower to watch a sundew beside the water's edge. The long reddish hairs on its leaves waved gently like welcoming arms. A fly landed, struggled to get free of the sticky goo, then slowly disappeared into the plant's innards.

She sat on the log and watched the lake for a long time, thinking about things that weren't what they seemed: smooth creamy mushrooms that were as lethal as a witch's poisoned apple, innocent-looking plants that were deathtraps in disguise, invisible afterdamp that could creep along the mineshaft and kill a man.

Her new dress no longer seemed new; it was stained with dirt and blood from picking up Danny when he fell and skinned his arm.

People weren't always what they seemed, either. Big, handsome Mr. Carpelli who was a fire boss and a Grand Knight in the Cavallotti Lodge had run away and hidden in the bush instead of facing up to his mates when it came to a showdown.

Sophia called herself a best friend, and she was to a point, except she was kind of stuck on herself. Lately it seemed as if the only reason she acted like a friend was to impress Jock.

And then there was Jock, so much like her father that it made Charlotte ache sometimes. He had a soft way of speaking and a tenor voice that put the rest of the cast of *The Mikado* to shame. And yet the men looked up to him, asked his advice, and appointed him spokesman at their meetings.

Somebody else who wasn't what he seemed was hovering at the edge of Charlotte's consciousness.

Then there was a rustle in the bushes, and a deer raised its head to look at her. Its brown eyes were soft and unblinking, and its whole being was breathlessly still, yet it seemed poised, ready to spring away at the slightest hint of danger. They looked at each other for a long time, and Charlotte saw something of her mother in the animal—the way it seemed to wait for a signal, some sign from the the guardian angels of the forest perhaps, before it decided what to do. Although she couldn't put it into words, she felt as though she had learned something very important about herself, about her mother, who often waited for a sign, too. Where did her sign come from? Her guardian angel?

She sighed deeply, leaned back against a tree trunk, half closed her eyes, and let her mind drift.

Nothing moved. There were no sounds, no whisper of wind in the trees, no calling of birds, or chirrup of insects. The air was as soft and quiet as Bea's imagined float among the stars.

But someone was standing on the path.

"Father," Charlotte whispered. He stood there wearing his Sunday-best suit with a sprig of forget-me-not in his lapel. But instead of a fedora, he wore his miner's cap, and the lamp was lit. It cast a soft glow over his face. He was trying to tell her something. His arms were out-stretched in a protective way she had seen many times when she was a little girl and he had soothed her after a fall, a disappointment, or a nightmare. She held her breath, afraid to move in case he left without speaking to her.

"Be careful, my little treasure," he seemed to say, and yet there was no sound in her ears.

"Careful of what, Father?" she asked. But he was gone, and she sat as if in a trance, savouring the feeling of his nearness, his caring.

SEVEN

Her reverie was interrupted by the pounding of foot-steps. Jock appeared around a bend in the path. His hair was windblown, and he looked anxious.

"There you are. I was worried about you. None of the others knew where you were."

"I'm fine, thank you," Charlotte said, looking into his lilac eyes. She thought she saw a faint reflection of her father walking away.

"You look all dreamy, girl. Were you sleeping then?"

"I don't think so." Charlotte felt as if she had been sleeping, though. Her feet didn't seem to be touching the ground, and the colours and sounds of the forest were so intense she could only gaze and listen as Jock helped her to her feet and walked back to the picnic with her.

She was glad they didn't stay for the dance. Her mother wanted to go home, and Bea and Danny were tired.

Jock left in a rowboat with some other men because they had something important to do, and it wasn't hard to guess what all the secrecy was about—the union, of course.

The image of her father beside the lake on Newcastle Island stayed with Charlotte. It had seemed so peaceful, she was sure it hadn't been a dream. She *had* seen him. He had come to let her know that everything was all right, but that she should be careful. She decided to make a list of all of the things she must be careful about, and she thought that if she got the right one he would let her know somehow.

1. At work. Be extra careful about rolling the dynamite.
2. Robert. Be as careful as I can about not letting him go into the mines, though I don't know how I can do that. Still, I'll look for a way.
3. Be careful about poison mushrooms and insect-eating plants, and things and people that look fine, but aren't.

She wished she could talk to her mother about guardian angels. Did she have one? She must. What else could it be when she went into a sort of trance? Did she see her husband? Did he tell her things?

One thing her father would want her to do, Charlotte decided, was to act more loving to her mother, even if she did call it "gushy." She thought about how hard it was for her mother to do all the cooking, washing, and cleaning by herself.

The next morning she felt awkward as she put an arm around her mother's shoulders and kissed her cheek before she left for work. "Don't overdo it today, Mum. I'll mix the bread when I get home."

Mabel stiffened for a brief second, saying, "My, aren't we being lovey today." Then she smiled and returned Charlotte's hug. "You be careful at work."

Charlotte finally got up enough nerve to ask Mr. Tweedsmuir why Sybil had quit her job. He seemed annoyed and told her she should let sleeping dogs lie. Then he asked her to change out of her coveralls before the next bookkeeping lesson. He said wearing a dress would make her feel more professional.

When Charlotte got home, the heavenly smell of newly baked bread greeted her before she was even in the door. "I said I'd do the bread, Mum." She kissed her mother's forehead.

Mabel shook her head. "No, Lottie, you've been on your feet all day. I won't have you coming home to more work."

Jock was sitting at the table, holding what Charlotte at first thought was the script for the play, but it was mimeographed and had the words *We Too* across the top.

"Why does it say *We Too*?" she asked. "Is it about the picnic and the boat taking us there?" She poured warm water from the reservoir on the side of the stove into the washbasin and reached for the soap.

"No, lass. This is a union bulletin. It's to tell the truth about the mines, the bosses, and how the dangers are worse because the company doesn't care about the men. There's more of a fracas when a mule dies than for a miner. We're handing it out to all the members, and one got nailed to a coal car and went right down into the mine." He laughed.

"But who did it? Who made it? And who drew that funny picture of James Dunsmuir?"

Robbie was sitting on the floor, legs spread, leaning against the Winnipeg couch and shooting marbles onto a small floor mat. He jumped up, looked over Jock's shoulder, and snorted when he saw the cartoon. "That's a good one. Looks just like the bloody bloke," he said, and went back to his solitary marble game.

Mabel half turned from the bread pans she was pulling from the oven and shook a floury forefinger at her son. "Robert, watch your tongue!"

"Do you know what was the last straw?" Jock asked. "The thing that really started this strike? Well, let me tell you. Two men were picked out of each mine to go around once or twice a month and check for gas. And if they found any, they were supposed to report it. So, in Extension two men reported gas and got fired on the spot. For reporting gas! Not only that, they were black-listed so they couldn't get a job anywhere else."

Bea looked up from a Grade Three primer. "Lottie, what does *delight* mean?"

"It means Bea is a dummy," Danny said, jumping up on the bench beside her and sticking out his tongue.

"Mother! Make Danny stop that. I'm trying to read, and he's being pesky."

"Daniel, leave your sister alone," Mabel ordered.

"Hey, Danny, you can butter my bread," Charlotte said. "You do it so nicely."

Danny spent the next eight minutes buttering a

thick slice of warm bread, his tongue sticking out of the corner of his mouth, his eyes narrowed in concentration.

"Are you coming to the play?" Jock asked Charlotte and her mother.

"But what does it mean, *delight*?" Bea interrupted.

"Joy, extra-special happiness, that's what it means," Jock said. "Beatrice the Beautiful."

Beatrice grinned and scrunched her chin into her collar. "Aw, quit that."

"Don't breathe a word to a soul that I showed you *We Too*," Jock said.

"No, never, lad." Charlotte's mother turned hot loaves out of the pans, wiped her hands on her apron, and dished up a steaming plate of boiled cabbage and stewed rabbit for Charlotte. "Sit and eat, Lottie. You must be starved."

Jock was giving Danny bread-buttering instructions. He pointed. "You missed a wee spot. There."

"When is it to be? Your play?" Mabel asked. "I've a good mind to go. Bea and Danny might like it."

"July 18, a fortnight Friday. I'll get tickets, so you needn't pay. Charlotte, will you come?"

Charlotte had managed to avoid thinking about *The Mikado* for a long time. She had been to only two rehearsals before dropping out, and had resolutely pushed aside the picture of smiling faces and bantering voices at rehearsals every Tuesday night.

"I'm not sure," she said.

"Please?"

"All right. Yes, of course I'll go."

❦

Jock was a different person onstage than off. He had learned his part well, and his tenor voice was perfect for the lighthearted performance.

Sophia was pretty yummy as Yum Yum, too. She was a little heavy on her feet for a Japanese girl; still, her voice wasn't bad and her acting was very expressive. It hardly seemed like acting at all, the way Sophia did it. The whole thing was good, right to the very last song, even though Charlotte's arms ached from holding Danny, who slept through the last fifty minutes.

Charlotte was glad she hadn't worn her new dress. She had thought it wouldn't help to make her feel she was anywhere near as important or pretty as the actresses, and she had been right about that.

Jock and Sophia got a standing ovation when they came out for their curtain call.

Later that night Charlotte was too restless to sleep. Bea was dead to the world. She looked like an angel, with her hair spread out on the pillow. She was an angel, Charlotte thought. A sweet-tempered child.

The Mikado had been extra-good. She wished she could have been in it. It would have been fine to be Katisha, or one of the schoolgirls, or in the chorus. But, she decided firmly, she might as well not think about being in plays or anything like that. Her job and earning money were the most important things in the world. Maybe she should stop singing in the church choir, too. She knew most of the hymns, so it didn't matter much if she couldn't go to practice, but it would probably be best if she dropped out.

She kept thinking about her father. A lot of the time it seemed as if he were with her, trying to keep her safe. She was trying extra-hard to be careful, as he had said.

But, strangely, she noticed that as soon as she went into Mr. Tweedsmuir's office he seemed to leave her. Why was that?

🐑

Usually the morning walk from the train stop down to the dynamite plant was alive with sound: birds sang, men whistled and joked, girls chattered, and Chinese workers conversed in singsong voices. It was the best time of the day. At shift's end the hike was harder going because it was uphill, and everybody was too tired to joke, laugh, or whistle.

On July 21 the walk seemed different. The road ahead was hidden in a thick grey fog, and Charlotte felt a prick of anxiety as she picked her way along, being careful not to step on slugs, listening for other voices. The surrounding forest was quiet, and the air seemed hard to breathe.

Surely she couldn't be late, but why was nobody else going to work? She was relieved to find, when she arrived, that other people were there, some ahead of her, some behind. Voices were lost in the mist, but the foghorn from Entrance Lighthouse sent eerie moans across the strait.

Then Mr. Tweedsmuir materialized out of the grey wall. "Well, well, Charlotte, you look chipper this morning. Full of vim and vinegar, are we? This would be good time to have a little lesson, don't you think?"

Charlotte's feelings of apprehension increased. Mr. Tweedsmuir was reminding her of something, something connected with poison mushrooms and insect-eating plants, and that day beside the lake. Silly thought.

"Um, no, sir. You see, I have to get to my place or the others…"

He slipped his hand under her elbow and started to steer her toward the office. "Don't bother your pretty little head about the others. I'll look after them. There must be some advantage in being a friend of the boss, wouldn't you say?"

The foghorn called. Be careful, it seemed to say in her father's voice.

"No, sir. I have to go to work." Charlotte jerked her elbow away and hurried along the board sidewalk and plank runway to the packing and rolling house.

"Don't you like your job, girlie?" Mr. Tweedsmuir's voice called after her.

"Yes, sir, I do. Of course I like it." She stopped but didn't turn.

"Then, if I were you, I'd cooperate when someone with a lot of authority tries to teach you something new."

She turned slowly, but he had disappeared back into the fog.

Charlotte was in turmoil as she rolled dynamite. She was going to lose her job. Mr. Tweedsmuir had said as much. And it would be her own fault. What was the harm in letting him do her a favour? He was willing to make excuses for her to the other workers so she could learn bookkeeping. That was a better job than dynamite packing. He was only looking out for her interests, so why did she feel so anxious or depressed whenever she was in the office with him?

Maybe she could go and talk to him after work, be nice and apologize, and ask him politely not to fire her. With a flash, she suddenly remembered her grandmother's hands turning the pages of a book, pointing to a picture.

A picture that reminded her of Mr. Tweedsmuir. Fagin! A picture of Fagin in Charles Dickens's novel about Oliver Twist. A wicked old man who coaxed children off the streets and taught them to lie and steal and turned them into criminals for his own advantage. It all came together in Charlotte's mind. So this is what her father had warned her about.

Anger boiled up from the pit of Charlotte's stomach, and she could feel her face burning. So, Mr. Tweedsmuir wanted to teach her things for his own advantage, did he? She'd see about that!

But what could she do? Her heart sank. She *had* to keep her job. It was their only hope to get out of coal-mining towns forever. But she couldn't bear the thought of being alone with Mr. Tweedsmuir for one more second. She would be fired. No doubt about it. He would see to that if he couldn't have his way with her.

Tomorrow she would be back to scrubbing floors and doing other people's laundry, if she was lucky enough to get even those kinds of jobs. The strike was making things worse every day.

Charlotte thought about Sybil. Did she get fired? Was she scrubbing floors somewhere right now? Did she lose her job because she didn't cooperate?

What if Sybil...? What if Mr. Tweedsmuir...? She had to find out. Somehow or other, she simply must know what had happened to Sybil. Mr. Sykes knew, but he wouldn't tell. She must make him tell. She would find him during dinner break and persuade him to tell her what he knew.

EIGHT

Charlotte climbed down the steep cliff beside the narrow-gauge tracks under the tramway. The cars, operated by a winch, were used to haul powder from Chile up from the beach to the storage sheds, and to lower the dynamite back down to be shipped abroad.

She wasn't sure she would find Mr. Sykes on the beach, but he liked to beachcomb whenever he had a chance. He used the nice pieces of driftwood he picked up to make furniture.

The bay was full of sailing ships that looked like ghostly images of themselves in the fog-threaded air. A tall, slim smokestack to let the steam escape from the boiler used to generate electricity was attached with guy wires to four little concrete pyramids.

Charlotte moved along the beach, peering into the fog, hoping the hunchbacked figure of Mr. Sykes would be just around the next big boulder. And there he was. She sighed with relief.

"I canna say, lassie. I canna say wha' happened to the bonnie girl," he said to her when she asked him about Sybil.

"Please, Mr. Sykes, I must find out. You see..." Tears stung her eyes. "I'm going to get fired...and, and, I need the money." Charlotte blurted the words out and wished, not for the first time, that coveralls had pockets to carry handkerchiefs in. She rubbed her eyes with her knuckles.

Mr. Sykes looked at her and patted her shoulder awkwardly. "There, there, lass. Dinna carry on so." He turned to stare out toward the sea.

"I'm sorry. It's just." She hiccuped. "It's just that my father got killed in the mine, and my mother... We've got the little kids to take care of and I'm afraid." She gulped and took a deep breath. She would have to ask *the* question. Of course, it was brash beyond words for a girl to talk about such things to a man, especially a man she hardly knew, but she gathered her courage.

"Did Sybil—was she in the family way, do you know?"

Mr. Sykes looked uncomfortable, turned his head away, put his hand over his mouth, and gave a little cough. "Aye, leastwise that's what they be saying."

"So I guess he gave her money to go away." She thought he nodded, but she wasn't sure. "I won't tell anybody, Mr. Sykes. I promise I won't breathe a word about what you told me. Thank you." She wiped her hand on the side of her coveralls and held it out to shake. Then she climbed back up the hill and was pulling on her big boots just as the 12:30 whistle sounded the back-to-work warning.

Now that she knew the truth and her suspicions had been verified, she wasn't sure she was any better off. She would lose her job unless she agreed to go into the office on Sundays and holidays as Mr. Tweedsmuir had asked her to do.

At that moment a terrible roaring wind burst into her worried thoughts. *Bang!* A sound like a rifle shot. The building rocked back and forth. The wind sucked at the windows and they shattered. People screamed. Wooden shovels and packing cases flew through the air. Charlotte was on the floor and Runty was sprawled half on top of her. He groaned.

"Sweet Jesus, she's blown! Run for it!" a man's voice yelled.

But Charlotte couldn't move. She closed her eyes and prayed. "Dear God, please don't let Runty die." She tried to speak, but her mouth and nose were full of dust and powder.

Then Runty moved his head. "Are...you...alive?" he whispered.

"Yes." Charlotte didn't recognize her own voice. It was creaky and hoarse, and her tongue felt like a swollen bulb filling her mouth. "Are...you...all right?" she managed to ask.

"Dunno. Can't move."

"Don't try. They'll come and find us."

Charlotte closed her ears to the cries and moans of injured people and the sounds of breaking glass and shifting timbers and concentrated on Runty. He was pinned on top of her by a chunk of planking, and his head was bleeding. He must live. She must help him live. Just until help came. They *must* both be alive to be rescued.

She gathered her energy and struggled to make her voice sound steady. "We'll say the Twenty-third Psalm.

"'The Lord is my shepherd, I shall not want. He maketh me to lie down in green pastures: He leadeth me beside the still waters.'"

Charlotte felt something warm and sticky spreading across her chest. Blood. Her own or Runty's?

His arm moved.

"Hold on, Runty," Charlotte said. "'He restoreth my soul: He leadeth me in the paths of righteousness for His name's sake.'"

"Name's sake," Runty murmured.

"'Yea, though I walk through the valley of the shadow of death...' That's what we're doing, Runty. Are you with me? In the valley?"

"I be," he whispered.

"'I will fear no evil.'"

"No evil," Runty croaked, his voice a little stronger.

"'For Thou art with me; Thy rod and Thy staff...'"

Runty raised his shoulders, sucked in a deep breath, grunted, and collapsed back onto Charlotte's hips and stomach. Her feet were freezing, and numbness was creeping up her legs.

An eternity later, after Charlotte had finished the Twenty-third Psalm and insisted that Runty hum and moan along through eight hymns, including "Onward Christian Soldiers," "God Sees the Little Sparrow Fall," and "Amazing Grace," she stopped to think.

Runty's head jerked convulsively and was still.

"Are you with me?"

No answer.

"Runty!" She shifted her shoulders, trying to shake him.

Still no answer.

"Stay here!" she barked. "Don't you dare leave me! Don't you dare! Come on, Runty, we'll keep singing." She thought Runty moved, but she wasn't sure.

She stopped to listen. Were there voices outside? Yes. Voices. Heavy pounding footsteps. One voice recognizable above the others.

"Charlotte! Thank God, you're alive." Jock's face was above hers, his eyes darted around, and he was panting. "This way, men!" he yelled.

"We're saved, Runty, we're saved." Charlotte giggled feebly. But Runty didn't answer.

Charlotte closed her eyes and listened to the grunts and terse commands of the rescue team as the plank was heaved away. Half of her mind was filled with overwhelming gratitude—to God for being with her, and to these rough-and-tumble miners for finding her. The other half was filled with overwhelming dread about Runty. Was he alive or dead?

"He's alive," one of the miners said, "but just barely."

They lifted Runty, put him on the plank, covered him with a jacket, and carried him out.

"We'll be right back, as soon as we find some other blokes to take this one," one of the men who was carrying the makeshift stretcher said.

"Goodbye, Runty," Charlotte said, starting to cry. Runty wasn't a relative, or even a very close friend, but the hours of pain they had been through together had forged such a close bond that Charlotte thought she must die if he did.

Jock held her hand. "There, there, lass. Don't move.

Wait till the others come."

Tears streamed down Charlotte's face, and she stuffed her fist into her mouth, trying hard not to scream. Sobbing, she asked, "Is Runty...will he be..."

"I dinna know," Jock said, his strained voice taking on more of a burr.

There he went again, Charlotte thought. The more worried he was, the more he sounded like her father. So Scottish a body could scarcely understand.

"As soon as we get you out of here, I'll go to the hospital myself to look in on Runty," Jock promised.

"Oh, dear," Charlotte said. "What about Aw Lee?"

"Who?" Jock asked.

"Aw Lee—the Chinese man who works beside me"

"He must have got out. There's nobody else in here. But I'll find out for sure."

"Thank you!" Charlotte drew a deep, ragged breath, and suddenly she was as calm as the lake on Newcastle Island. Everything would be all right.

❧

It was so peaceful propped up in bed with the lamplight flickering and the smell of chicken soup wafting up the stairs. Charlotte was glad to be alive and happy that Runty was, too, even if he might be lame. Aw Lee was in the hospital with broken ribs, but nobody had been killed. She didn't think Runty would care much about being lame. He didn't seem to mind his cross eyes, or being so small, or having the kind of hair that always looked messy.

Bea was sleeping on the settee downstairs. Charlotte's mother had said she should have the bed to herself because of her bruises and scrapes. Although she did love Bea, it was nice to have so much room,

Mabel McEwan was pretty upset, and she had insisted that Charlotte quit her job immediately. Charlotte was sure she was going to get fired, anyway, although she didn't tell her mother that.

The plant was closed for repairs, but Charlotte was determined to go back to work as soon as it reopened. She had to have it out with Mr. Tweedsmuir. She had to figure out a way to both keep her job and stay away from that beastly man!

Charlotte heard a knock on the door downstairs. It was Jock. He seemed just as upset as her mother about the accident. He was asking all about her, how she felt, and if she had eaten anything. He sounded exactly like her father when she had had a bad case of the measles at the age of seven.

It was so nice to be alive and to have a friend like Jock who cared about her and her family. The bed, the quilt, the room, the house, and the whole world were just perfect, exactly the way everything should be. She wished she could feel like this forever.

Charlotte raised her head and straightened her back. She *would* return to the plant, and not just for the money. It was more than that.

Maybe some things were more important than danger. When she had been there with Runty, it had felt like the most important thing that had ever happened, and that if he didn't live then part of her would be dead, too. They had been connected as if they were one person, and she could feel his heart beating and his breathing. She had always thought Runty was just a funny-looking kid and not very smart about anything except dynamite. Maybe everybody in the whole world could be like that, caring as much for the other person as for themselves, if they had to be close to each other and think about dying. She would always care about Runty now. She would go to the hospital as soon as she could to see him. Maybe she would take the cribbage board and cards.

Everybody in the whole world caring about each other. That was a nice thought. But she was sure she could never in a million years feel like that about Mr. Tweedsmuir. Why was that? He was a person, too. Was it because he didn't care about Sybil, or her for that matter, except to have his own way? He was bigger, more important, and could hire and fire people, and he made people do what he wanted because of that. *Well, she wouldn't do what he wanted.* And she would figure out a way to keep her job, too.

❦

By the time the plant reopened, Charlotte's bruises had turned purple. Her face reminded her of Danny's squashed teddy bear. One cheek was swollen, one eye was half-closed, and a scab at the corner of her mouth hurt when she talked. She felt like a broken toy when she moved, too, but she could walk, and she was determined to go back to work.

"Lottie, you're not fit to go," her mother protested. "I don't mean about quitting the job. You're as set in your ways as your father was when it comes to that. I mean just now. Today. Wait a bit before you go back."

"I have to go, Mother. I have to do it right away." Should she tell her mother about Mr. Tweedsmuir? No. She wouldn't be fired, and that was a fact, and she wouldn't worry her mother any more than she had already done.

Mr. Sykes was standing guard at the gate as usual when Charlotte arrived on Thursday morning. "You look a proper sight, you do," he said, shaking his head and tsking. "You should be home abed until you get healed up proper like."

"No. I feel fine, Mr. Sykes. Honest I do. Have you heard if Runty will be coming back?"

"They already hired a new one to take his place."

"So what will happen to Runty?"

Mr. Sykes rubbed his back. "I been thinking for a spell now that it's time I leave. Got the rheumatism, you know."

"So you mean Runty might..."

"Aye. Directly he's back on his feet, I'll show him the ropes and they'll be glad enough to hire somebody who already knows it all. It's not as easy as you might think, this job."

Charlotte touched his arm. "Oh, Mr. Sykes, I'm sure it's not easy. Thank you so much. Runty needs a job badly."

The old man smiled and nodded. "You're a good lass. A bonnie girl you are."

When she got to her station, Charlotte hummed a song from *The Mikado* as she worked: "'Three little maids from school are we, dah, dah, dee, dah, dah, dah dee dee.'"

A young woman Charlotte had never seen before entered the shed hesitantly and moved to Runty's place. "Are you Charlotte?" she asked.

Charlotte nodded. "What's your name?"

"Ingrid."

Ingrid was very pretty, Charlotte thought, aware of her own bruised and misshapen face.

"Does it hurt?" Ingrid asked, a worried look on her face. "Did you fall down?"

Charlotte patted her cheek lightly. "Oh, no. It happened when they had that explosion at the nitrator."

Ingrid had strawberry-blond curly hair, wide-set blue eyes, and smooth, pale skin.

Charlotte was so busy showing Ingrid how to roll the sticks just right, like cigars, that she wasn't aware of Mr. Tweedsmuir's approach until he was standing behind them.

"How are you feeling, Charlotte? Better, my dear?" He looked at her. For a split second the smile on his face changed to a look of revulsion, and then the smile was back. Obviously he wasn't interested in her, looking as she did today. So that would be the secret: look ugly all the time and he wouldn't bother her.

Mr. Tweedsmuir leaned toward the new girl, patting her hand, smiling his phony smile. "If you have any problems now, anything at all you don't understand or would like help with, you be sure to come to me, won't you, Ingrid?" His voice was soothing and low.

Charlotte felt sure she should warn Ingrid about Mr. Tweedsmuir, but how? Maybe she should just wait a little while. Ingrid might realize for herself what was going on with him. But Charlotte knew she would feel horrible if Ingrid fell into Mr. Tweedsmuir's trap. She concentrated on her words.

"Ingrid?"

Ingrid looked alarmed. "Am I doing it wrong?"

"No, no. You're doing it right, but there's something I should tell you. Mr. Tweedsmuir, he's not—he's not as nice as he seems. Do you know what I mean?"

Ingrid looked puzzled. "I'm not sure. Is he cruel to the workers?"

"No. But he tries to coax me to go into the office and promises to teach me bookkeeping, and the girl who worked here before had to go away because..." Charlotte could feel herself blushing and turned away.

She felt the light touch of Ingrid's hand on her shoulder and heard a whispered word she didn't understand.

NINE

On her way home from work, Charlotte saw Robbie in a gang of youths, all with empty kerosene cans tied around their necks. They were following a group of women to the post office and yelling, "Scabbie. Dirty scab. Dirty scab," as they banged on the cans. The women looked terrified, even though they were being escorted by policemen. These were women whose husbands had gone back to work, and Charlotte couldn't help but feel sorry for them. Sometimes a man didn't have much choice.

She called to Robbie, but he lifted his chin defiantly and said, "I gotta do somethin' to help. Father would if he was still alive."

Yes. He would do something to help, but not terrify

innocent women and children. Charlotte sighed. She would have to have a serious talk with Robbie and try to make him understand.

The strike was spreading, and Jock was no longer living with the Trimbles. He was gaining a reputation as a fiery pro-union activist and was afraid the strike-breakers would do something terrible to the Trimbles' house if he stayed.

The problem with Mr. Tweedsmuir was soon back. Ingrid didn't come back to work after the first day, and Charlotte heard she had quit. Charlotte's face was all better, so she looked like herself again. Mr. Tweedsmuir came over to say she had better go in on Sunday to resume her bookkeeping lessons. Charlotte said she couldn't do that, but he said she better think long and hard about it.

So the old worries about losing her job returned, only worse. She tried to remember how she had been after the accident, with the feeling that everything was all right. All she knew for sure was that she wouldn't go into the office ever again, and she would keep her job, even if she had to do something sneaky. She had heard her father say you had to fight fire with fire, so what kind of fire could she use on Mr. Tweedsmuir?

She wished she could ask Jock. He was very good at strategy, as the miners called it. But she didn't see how she could ask him without mentioning certain things she wouldn't dare talk about, even to her mother.

The conflict between the miners and the strike-breakers was escalating. The strikebreakers were living in boarding houses right in town now, and quite a few of the regulars were returning to work and moving back into their own homes. That meant trouble with a capital *T*.

The McEwans were lucky in a way; no miners lived in their house, so they were left in peace. But it was an uneasy peace. There was so much yelling, gunshots, and commotion that they could scarcely sleep at night. Gangs of strikers were out throwing stones at houses and putting up signs: GO HOME SCABBIE and DIRTY BLACKLEG. They called them Black Minorcas, too. Charlotte didn't know why, but Jock told her it was the name of a kind of chicken.

Police were everywhere, and there were rumours that the army would be brought in. Charlotte wished she knew where Jock was staying. He hadn't been around for quite a while, and she missed him. She felt better when she went off to work knowing he was looking out for her family. She just hoped and prayed neither Jock nor Robbie would get hurt. Or killed.

❦

"Runty! I'm so glad to see you." Charlotte rushed toward him where he was guarding the gate at the dynamite plant and shook his hand.

He grinned and doffed his cap. "Mornin', Charlotte. We had us a bad one, didn't we? I can still hear your voice. All those hymns. You just kept on asingin' and asingin'. 'Onward Christian so-o-o-ol-jer-r-rs,'" he sang off-key, smiling.

Charlotte joined in. "'Marching as to war.'" She smiled back.

Runty stopped smiling and looked at her solemnly. "Charlotte," he began, and then broke off. "Charlotte," he tried again, turning and staring into the distance. "Mr. Sykes, he's been tellin' me a few things I don't like the sound of." His voice was so low that Charlotte could barely hear him. He looked down and scuffed the toe of his boot on the ground.

Charlotte put a hand on his arm. "What's he been telling you, Runty?" Then she knew. "About Sybil?" she asked quietly.

Runty nodded. "So I just wanted to tell you, Charlotte. I'm around all the time. You get in any scrapes, you just yell for me, you hear?" He studied her anxiously.

"Thanks, Runty, I will. Has Mr. Sykes left altogether then? Are you the watchman now?"

"More or less. He comes in the evening for a hot cuppa tea and a chin wag in the bunkhouse. Kinda cheers me on, makes sure I'm on top of things." He shook his head. "A real honourable fella, he is. Real honourable. Like you, Charlotte." He blushed and turned away.

"You're a real honourable fellow, too, Runty." She swallowed the lump in her throat as she hurried along the boardwalk to work.

"Don't forget what I told you," he called after her.

So Mr. Sykes was worried enough about her to tell Runty, and Runty was worried enough about her to offer to be her bodyguard. She would have to face up to Mr. Tweedsmuir once and for all.

She didn't have long to wait for an opportunity. Two days later, as she was the last to leave the washhouse, Mr. Tweedmuir called to her. "Missy! I'd like to have a word with you." He was standing in front of the office with the door open behind him.

Charlotte stopped. "Yes, sir?"

"Come here," he beckoned.

Charlotte hesitated. Should she go? As far as she knew, everyone else had left the plant. She hadn't been expecting to face up to him with no one else in the whole place. She glanced anxiously toward the gate, hoping to see Runty on guard, but he wasn't there.

Mr. Tweedsmuir walked slowly toward her. "I said I'd like to have a word with you." He was smiling, but his voice sounded cold and tight.

"I'm sorry. I've got to go." Charlotte turned and hurried toward the exit.

"You're fired!"

The words hit like an explosion—almost as terrifying as the day the plant had blown up. They say dying people see their past lives flash before their eyes, but Charlotte saw her future: a life of drudgery and fear. Robbie would go down into the mines. Beatrice would marry a man who would go down into the mines. Danny would go down into the mines. Her mother would die of a broken heart when one, or the other, or all three of them were killed.

She stiffened, then turned and started to walk toward him, her head bowed. She had to buy some time. She must convince him that she would do his bidding some other day. And then what? Make a plan? Hadn't she wracked her brain trying to think of something at least a thousand times during the past month?

"There's a good girl," Mr. Tweedsmuir said soothingly. "Just come into the office so we can have a little talk."

Charlotte pulled back. "No, please. Couldn't we talk some other day? Couldn't I just keep working for now, and I'll come in on a Sunday like you say and learn what it is you want to teach me?"

He put his arm around her waist. "Come on, love. Now's as good a time as any."

Charlotte shivered.

"Don't be afraid. Just give us a little kiss. That won't

hurt you, will it?" He reached for her hand. "You can keep your job. In fact, better than that, I'll make you my assistant. Assistant bookkeeper. How would you like that, eh? Double the salary. Half the work. How about it?"

Charlotte wanted to scream and run, but she knew she mustn't panic. Keep calm, she told herself. Look for a way, any way, to put him off.

They were near the office door. "So was this how it was with Sybil?" she asked.

His face blanched, and he stopped moving, staring at her. "What are you talking about?"

"Sybil had to leave town, didn't she? I wonder what Mrs. Tweedsmuir would say if she knew."

His face was contorted. "Who do you think you are? Your word against mine? Come on, silly little girl, where's you brain?" He looked over Charlotte's shoulder and scowled. "What are you doing here?" he snarled.

"Just doing my job. Checking to see things are on the up-and-up." It was Runty's voice, and Charlotte thought she would faint with relief.

Runty was holding a chunk of steel pipe. For several seconds the only sound was that of Mr. Tweedsmuir's breathing.

Finally Runty spoke. "I'll kill you if need be," he said, and held the steel weapon above his head. "Let her be."

"You're both fired!" Mr. Tweedsmuir roared. "Don't you dare set foot on this property again!"

"Leave, Charlotte," Runty said. "Go."

Charlotte shuffled backward to stand behind Runty. "No. I'm not leaving you alone here. Not with him. He might have a gun."

"We gotta knock him out then, don't we?" Runty said matter-of-factly.

"I don't have a gun," Mr. Tweedsmuir whined. "Just go."

"Naw. Sorry," Runty said, shaking his head. "You'll try somethin' funny. Get over here where I can get a better swing at you." He pointed. "Stand back, Charlotte." He fingered the steel pipe.

Mr. Tweedsmuir moved to where Runty was pointing. "I don't have a gun, honest to God. Just lock me in the office and take the key with you."

"Where's the key?"

"In my pocket."

"Could do that," Runty said. "Easier to knock you out and be done with it." He seemed to be enjoying himself.

"Look, I promise you won't be fired. You can both stay on. Just lock me in, please."

"I'd rather trust a rattlesnake," Runty said contemptously. "You're a low-down rat, mister."

"But I mean it. Honest to God!" Mr. Tweedsmuir clasped his hands and gazed into Runty's face.

"Well... Charlotte, grab that jimmy bar," Runty said without taking his eyes off Mr. Tweedsmuir.

She did as she was told.

"Stay behind me. And use it if you have to." He moved a small step forward and said, "Now throw that key over."

Mr. Tweedsmuir's hand shook as he fished a key from his pant pocket and tossed it to Runty, who caught it with one hand.

"Let's get outta here." Runty slammed the office door and locked it. "You go ahead, Charlotte. I can't run as fast as you."

"No. We're staying together."

"Then follow me. We'll go through the bush, just in case the guy gets outta there."

But Mr. Tweedsmuir didn't get "outta" there for over

an hour. Runty was at Mr. Sykes's house explaining why he couldn't guard the plant that night. Mr. Sykes said not to worry. He would go down for a day or two until they saw which way the wind was blowing. "I'm not afraid of that man," he said.

🛒

Charlotte's arm was scratched and her breath came in little gasps.

"Why, Lottie, whatever is the matter? You look like you've just seen a ghost," her mother said.

"Come upstairs, Mum. I need to tell you something private."

She sat on the bed, and her mother joined her. "Lottie, whatever in the world is the matter?"

Charlotte clasped her cheeks in her hands and stared at the floor. "It's Mr. Tweedsmuir. He tried to make me go into the office after everybody else had left," she mumbled.

Mabel's voice was sharp and angry. "He what? He tried to get you alone in the office with nobody else around?"

"Yes. Runty was there, but he didn't know that."

"And what happened?" Mabel demanded. "Did he touch you?"

"No. You see, Mr. Sykes sort of warned me, and he told Runty. Runty said he'd look out for me, and he did. He did, Mum." Charlotte put her arms around her mother's neck and started to cry.

Mabel held her and patted her back. "There, there, Charlotte. The man's a dirty bounder, that's what he is. He should be tarred and feathered."

Charlotte reached for a handkerchief and blew her nose. "Mr. Sykes let it out that Sybil, who used to work there, had to leave town because she was in the family way."

"Because of him?"

Charlotte nodded.

"What a disgraceful thing! How did you get away from him?"

"Runty came running up holding a piece of iron and said he would kill him if he didn't leave me alone. Then he locked him in the office while we got away."

"It's a terrible thing," her mother said angrily. "What a blessing that Mr. Sykes and Runty were watching out for you."

"I know. I feel like Runty saved my life. And Mr. Sykes, too."

Mabel stood and pulled Charlotte up. "Thank God for that. You did the right thing, Lottie. Don't you ever blame yourself for what that nasty man tried to do. You need a cup of tea and something to eat."

The next day was Saturday, and Charlotte didn't go to work, but she was determined to have it out with Mr. Tweedsmuir. Her mother was just as determined that the only way she would even think of allowing such a thing was if she went along herself and threatened him. She wasn't one to spread gossip, but she would spread this gossip far and wide and do her best to see that he was run out of town if she ever heard of him so much as laying a finger on Charlotte or any other young girl.

A neighbour woman came in to get Beatrice off to school and mind Danny on Monday morning, and Charlotte's mother, wearing her best black skirt, a high-necked lace blouse, her tweed coat, and a black hat with a short veil, clenched her hands and clamped her mouth shut as they approached the plant. Mr. Sykes was guarding the gate, and Charlotte's heart sank. Had something awful happened to Runty?

"Runty's not here," she said anxiously as she grabbed her mother's arm and hurried her along. She ran the last two hundred yards. "Where's Runty?" she gasped.

"Don't worry yourself, lassie. He's right as rain," Mr. Sykes said.

"Oh, thank heaven," Charlotte said with a deep sigh.

Mr. Sykes grinned and patted the top of her head. "Tweedsmuir ain't coming back,"

Charlotte stared, wide-eyed. "He's not?"

Mr. Sykes winked. "Seems he got transferred. One of the owners got wind of what was going on. Runty's keeping an eye on things until the new manager gets here."

Charlotte put an arm around his shoulders. "Oh, Mr. Sykes, you're just the best friend. I'm so happy." She clapped her hands and did a little jig. "Runty stood up for me against Mr. Tweedsmuir, you know."

Mr. Sykes nodded. "I know all about it." He leaned closer. "But Runty said you was standin' up for yourself pretty good, lassie. That's what I like—a gal with spirit."

In her agitation Charlotte had forgotten to introduce her mother and she did so now. "Mr. Sykes, I'd like you to meet my mother." She took her mother's elbow and pulled her forward.

Mr. Sykes doffed his cap. "How do. That's a mighty fine girl you got there Miz McEwan."

Mabel shook his hand firmly. "Indeed she is. I'm proud of her. I want to thank you for looking out for her. And Runty, too. Will you tell him?"

"Aye, to be sure I will."

Mabel smiled and reached into the bag she was carrying. "I brought you and Runty a little something to have with your tea, just a wee appreciation for what you did for our Lottie." She handed over a parcel.

"Why thankee. Thankee very much," Mr. Sykes said. "She deserves lookin' after, that one does."

Charlotte walked partway up the hill with her mother. "I told you Mr. Sykes was nice, didn't I, Mum?"

"Yes, he is very nice, Lottie"

"What was in the parcel?"

"Just a cherry cake."

"A cherry cake? Oh, Mum, that's the perfect thing for Runty and Mr. Sykes. Thank you." Charlotte hugged her mother as she said goodbye. "It's going to be ever so nice to work without worrying about Mr. Tweedsmuir coming in," she called over her shoulder as she hurried back to the plant. She hummed as she pulled on her work boots and went into the packing and rolling house.

TEN

The shutters on the train were open, and Charlotte leaned her head out and watched and listened with increasing appprehension on the ride home. She seemed to be moving inexorably from the outer edges into the very centre of a terrible disaster.

At the Nanaimo stop strikers waited to tell triumphantly about what they had done to those scabs who had been working in the South Wellington mine. "We rounded them up, marched them down to the wharf, and sent them packing. Couple of dozen special police were gettin' off the ferry. We were five hundred strong, and we sent them back where they come from. We were none too gentle with them."

A boy on horseback came galloping along the street,

yelling at the top of his lungs. "Six men killed in Extension! Six men shot! It's in the newspaper! Six men dead!"

Miners cursed and shook their fists, raising their weapons in the air. "Come on, brothers. This is bloody murder. To Extension!"

The word echoed in Charlotte's head like some terrible curse.

Extension-tension-tension. Her blood ran cold. Six men killed. Was Jock one of them?

She must not scream or cry out. With her jaw clamped shut, she sat on her hands.

The train started to move again, and she strained her eyes, hoping to see Jock among the gangs of men. She caught glimpses of the wagon road, choked with traffic. There were men on horseback, in wagons, marching along on foot—singing, yelling, carrying guns and axes and baseball bats.

As the train drew closer to Extension, it got worse. Many of the windows of homes they passed that had always revealed lamplit glimpses of family life—people gathering at the supper table, a woman dishing up food—were black and lifeless. She could see women and children running into the forest clutching blankets and clothing.

Her throat was tight with fear as she got off the train. The miners from Nanaimo were being hailed and greeted by the Extension strikers. "Come on, brothers. We'll rush the pithead." She saw a searchlight picking out one house after another—the houses of the men who had gone back to work.

Was Jock dead? Would her family be gone, running like frightened animals into the woods? What of Robbie?

Was he out there in the chaos?

The hill into town was black with marching men, and the sounds of loud and raucous voices yelling insults and oaths made her cringe as she got off the train. She stood still and took stock of the situation.

"Hey, there! You! Any filthy scabs in your family?" A boy scarcely older than Robbie ran toward her, carrying an axe and waving a box of matches.

"Leave her be! Her father was killed in the bloody mine." It was Jock's voice. "This way, Charlotte." He put an arm around her and hurried her along the road toward her home.

His face was bruised, his hand was bleeding, and his voice was hoarse and anxious. "It's a sorrowful time and getting worse. There'll be blood in the streets before this night is over. You have to promise me one thing, Charlotte. Stay inside. Don't light any lamps."

"But what if Mother and the little kids aren't there? What if Robbie's not home?"

"We'll see to that when we get there. Now hurry."

At first Charlotte thought the house was empty, and she tried the door. It was barred from the inside. Then her mother called out, "Lottie? Thank the Lord you're home."

"Where's Robbie?" Charlotte asked.

"He's safe and sound, except for a sprained ankle. I hope he's learned his lesson good and proper." Her mother held Danny in one arm and had her other around Beatrice, who was whimpering and clinging to her skirts.

"You all stay in now, hear?" Jock said. "They won't torch this place. Or the Trimbles' neither, with an invalid in there." He looked down, shook his head, wiped his brow with the back of his hand, and was gone.

Charlotte was reminded of how she had felt when she was trapped under the beam with Runty. What had seemed appropriate then might be appropriate now. She took several deep breaths and said, "Come on, we'll sing hymns." But the singing didn't work this time. It was bedlam out there.

Robbie sat on a chair with his bandaged foot raised on a stool and looked out the window, fingering a baseball bat. He sounded like a sports announcer as he gave a running report of the events in an excited voice. "They're up on the ridge, must be hundreds of them.... They're starting to shoot at the pithead. Woo-ee, listen. Bullets are flying all over the place."

"God be with us," Charlotte's mother whispered.

Danny broke away from his mother and huddled in a corner with his arms over his head. "Are we going to get shot?" he asked between sobs.

Charlotte lifted him and hugged him. "No, no. Hush now. We'll be all right. Jock will make sure they don't hurt us."

Jock would make sure? she thought. How on earth could he make sure of that? But the idea seemed to comfort Danny.

"Come and look at the searchlight, Danny," Robbie said. "See. That house over there that's burning belongs to one of the bloody scabs."

"Bloody scabbies," Danny parroted.

Mabel stopped rocking. "Robbie, watch your—" But she broke off and waved her hand dismissively. "Never mind." She seemed to decide that anything that would calm Danny down, including bad words, was worth the price.

"Look, up the road," Danny said. "They're smashing

the windows. They're going into Mr. Campbell's house. Nobody's home. How come they're smashing windows? Look, they're taking stuff out. Mrs. Campbell's best clock. And the baby's crib. How come they can take stuff, Robbie?"

Mabel came to life. She moved to look out the window with her hand on Danny's head and said, "It's wrong, son. It's a sin."

"They asked for it!" Robbie shouted.

Mabel was angry. She shook her finger in Robbie's face as she spoke. "Women and helpless little children asked to be chased out of their homes? Their houses set on fire? Their treasures stolen? Listen, my lad, fighting in the streets is bad enough, but setting fires and looting are mighty close to being the worst sins of mankind."

"Yes, ma'am. Look, they're headin' back the other way." Robbie sounded disappointed. "I'd have stood up to them." He raised the bat in a threatening way.

"Of course you would," his mother said. "You would have protected us as well as you were able. But protecting your family and going out looking for trouble are two very different things, Robert. Certainly it's all right to fight for a cause. I'm not denying that. The miners deserve a whole lot better than they've been getting—better pay, safer working conditions, and the rest. And they've got to stick to their demands, too. But a lot of those hoodlums out there aren't even sixteen yet. They're fighting for the thrill of it. It won't settle a thing, mark my words. There are other ways besides shooting and burning."

All night long they heard gunshots and shouts and smelled burning wood. Anxiety such as Charlotte had never known filled her heart. Death was one thing. Terrible as it was, at least it was final. This paralyzing fear clutching her was different. Not fear for her own safety. It was fear for someone else. Did one of those singing bullets have Jock's number on it, as she had heard men say about war? She prayed with all her might that Jock's number wasn't on any of the bullets that terrorized the village during that long night.

It was a bad riot, but nobody was killed. The *Nanaimo Free Press* posted a notice in its window that nine men were killed in Extension, but it wasn't true. At least that was something to be thankful for, but there wasn't much else to be happy about.

Eleven houses were burned in Extension, as well as the mine buildings and the manager's home. Some of the embers were still smoking, and black piles of horrible garbage were heaped where neighbours' houses used to be. All their worldly goods had disappeared in one night.

Soon after the August 13 riot, news spread that officials were making lists of people to arrest. On the night of August 20, twelve hundred miners gathered for a union meeting in Nanaimo, and the army was ready. Soldiers surrounded the hall and ordered the men out six at a time, single file. Rows of soldiers on both sides with fixed bayonets herded the men to the court house where they were searched for weapons. Forty-three were arrested. The McEwans were relieved to learn that Jock wasn't one of them.

He was arrested a few days later, however, as the roundup continued. In many homes there was a knock on the door in the middle of the night. Soldiers were there to arrest the men in the house, including boys of sixteen.

When asked for a warrant for the arrests, they said, "We haven't got a warrant. We don't need one under martial law."

During those few days, one hundred and seventy-nine men were arrested. They were all strikers or sympathizers. Not a single strikebreaker was among them.

Charlotte decided to persuade her mother to visit Jock in jail. She couldn't go alone; it wouldn't be proper. How long would he be in? she wondered. Until he rotted, as people sometimes said? The union was attempting to put up bail, so Charlotte tried to look on the bright side. But it was hard. She couldn't see any bright side, or any end to it at all. And visiting the jail to see Jock certainly didn't make the situation look any brighter.

The court house was elegant with wide halls tiled in a black-and-white fleur-de-lis pattern and big mahogany doors with leaded glass windows leading into spacious offices. Halfway down the hallway was a plain small wooden door. Charlotte gasped as the guard opened the door and she looked down a narrow wooden stairway flanked by solid brick walls to the concrete floor below. There was an iron door at the bottom of the stairs and just barely enough space for a passageway between two cells, each with a small barred window. Another door at the end of the passageway led directly outside, and this was where the prisoners were brought in. It was like a dungeon, and Charlotte shivered as she peered through the bars, looking for Jock.

Then her heart sank. The person she found there wasn't Jock. An unshaven face peered out. This man belonged in the slums of London, along with Fagin and his thieving boys. His clothing was stained, his eyes stone-grey and dull in the faint light. He clutched the bars of the cell with both hands, his mouth clamped tightly shut. Then he smiled. "Charlotte! Mrs. McEwan!"

The voice was his, and the smile was his, but surely

there must be some mistake. This couldn't be the laughing, confident man she knew, who could sing like Enrico Caruso and make Beatrice blush with his teasing.

As Charlotte's eyes became accustomed to the half-light, she could see into the cell. The room was six by ten by eight feet high, and Jock wasn't alone. There were three bunks one on top of another, and two of them were occupied. One man, in the top bunk, was reading a magazine; another sat in the lower bunk with his feet on the floor. They were both grinning and eyeing Charlotte.

Jock reached one hand through the bars, then pulled it swiftly back. "I'm so glad you came."

"We brought you a blackberry pie." Charlotte said. "I picked the fruit out beside the creek yesterday after work. But they wouldn't let me bring it in. Anyway, I don't know how we could have got it through the bars, without the juice all running away." She fiddled nervously with her handbag. "Unless we cut it up. Or maybe we could have put it in a jar with a lid. We didn't bring a jar with a lid. Oh, dear!" She smacked the palm of her hand against her forehead. "Why didn't we think to sneak it by in a jar with a lid?" She couldn't keep the tears out of her voice.

Jock chuckled and looked at her. "Maybe because you never tried to pass a pie through jail bars before, lassie." His eyes were mauvy-blue again, and he was the same old Jock. "Don't look so worried." He leaned close to the bars and spoke softly. "It's not so bad. Word has it that we should be out before long."

Charlotte pulled a handkerchief from her pocket and sniffled into it. "I'm glad."

"And the guards will get a rare treat with their tea,"

Jock said. "Blackberry pie." He patted his stomach.

"But I picked the berries for you. Every one has got your name on it." And that was the truth. She had been so thankful none of the bullets fired on the night of the riot had had Jock's name on it that she had mentally written his name on every berry as she picked it.

"And that's all the pie I need," Jock said. "Just to know you were thinking of me is more than enough. Don't worry. It will turn out all right. You'll see. It's a real treat to see you. There's no mistaking that. But it's best you don't come again. I'm afraid they'll put you out of your house for being in cahoots with the likes of me." He looked as if he was trying hard to keep smiling, and he rubbed his forearms with his hands as he spoke. "I'll write you a letter," he whispered. "But don't write back. They open our mail."

Charlotte blinked back tears, smiled, and held her head high as she walked back up the stairs.

ELEVEN

To Charlotte, looking out of the train on her way to work the next day, it seemed like a country at war. Soldiers patrolled the streets. They had set up camp in strategic positions so that anyone entering or leaving Nanaimo would get the message. Tents, horses, arms, ammunition, and a large gun mounted on a flat car announced the new regime. Attorney General Bowser had brought one thousand men of the Seventy-Second Regiment to the island, and no sooner had a few people gathered in the streets than they were dispersed by "Bowser's Seventy-Two."

Robbie had taught her a song about them the evening before, and she sang it to herself as she walked down the hill to Departure Bay.

Oh, did you see the kiltie boys,
Well, laugh, 'twould nearly kilt you, boys,
That day they came to kill both great and small
With bayonet, shot, and shell, to blow you all to hell.
A dandy squad was Bowser's seventy-twa.

They stood some curious shapes these boys,
They must have sprung from apes these boys,
Dressed up in kilts to represent the law,
Ma conscience it was grand, hurrah for old Scotland,
And Bowser with his gallant seventy-twa.

"Morning, Charlotte." The new plant manager always stood outside to greet the workers as they arrived. Some said it was because he was watching for latecomers, but Charlotte preferred to think it was because he liked to "run a tight ship," as he often said. Running a tight ship was fine with her. She liked to work hard and feel satisfied that she was giving value for the money she earned.

But it was hard to concentrate today. There were a lot of things on her mind.

Extension was no less a war zone than Nanaimo. Charlotte had seen the little hut at the entrance to Old Number One. A sentry stood guard day and night. No one was allowed into the area, except for the strikebreakers and Robbie. He said they didn't bother about kids, and maybe he was right. He said he went because he liked the mules. He could brush and feed the animals, and he had asked for permission to exercise them.

Robbie had often begged for a dog, so perhaps the mules were like pets to him. Charlotte hoped fervently that was what it was all about and that her brother wasn't up to mischief.

But there were other things to worry about. The well was running dry. Her mother would have to do the washing at the creek until the rains started.

Actually, laundry day at the creek wasn't that much of a hardship. Some of Charlotte's happiest early memories were of those times. It was a community affair: several families went together and took the kids and picnic lunches and made a day of it.

A few women would go early to light the fires between two walls made of rocks cemented together. Then the others would arrive, carrying dirty laundry in big baskets. They scooped water from the creek and filled the tubs. There were three washings. The first water was the dirtiest, the second was cleaner, and then everything was put in the washboiler to boil. They lifted it out piece by piece with sticks, dropped it into the cold rinse water, wrung it out, and took it home to hang. The pit clothes were never done on the same day as the other things, so dry wells meant two days a week at the creek.

Charlotte almost wished she could be there, but the one big difference between washing clothes and rolling and wrapping dynamite was that she got paid for the latter. She reminded herself of that several times during the long hot day.

When Charlotte returned home from work, she found that her mother had made a stew and mashed potatoes for supper. "This tastes better than anything else in the world I can think of right now," Charlotte said. "Thanks, Mum. Danny's right. You really are a good cook. The best in Extension, to be sure."

"Nonsense," Mabel said. "It's just plain food. You're hungry, is all." She started to fold laundry and stack it at the end of the table.

Charlotte took a big swallow of milk. "Mmm, the clothes smell nice." It had always seemed to her that the creek laundry was cleaner and sweeter-smelling than any other.

"How was it at the creek today? Were there quite a few there?"

Mabel nodded. "Three policemen came with us. Seems when you've got military law even the womenfolk and children might be dangerous if they're allowed to go about their business. They call it protecting, but protecting who? The strikebreakers are the ones getting protected. You can't even stop on the street to talk to a neighbour before a policeman or a soldier tells you to move along.

"We got rid of the policemen, though. Told them we saw three bears just over the hill heading for Mount Benson." She laughed. "They got all excited about that. 'Come on, lads. Let's go git us a bear rug,' they said. We never did see them again." Mabel's voice took on a serious tone. "Did you know they had the big court case yesterday?"

"They did? I thought it was next week. Was Jock there?"

"No. He's been sent to Victoria along with the others from Ladysmith and Extension. It was too crowded to keep them all here."

"Do you think he'll be all right, Mum? In Victoria?" Charlotte's asked, her voice faltering.

"Of course he will, and he won't be there long. They'll all be coming back here for their trial. He's a good strong lad, and a determined one. I know the men need to do what they're doing to try to make the company treat them decently, but it's a terrible hardship on everybody. And Jock is a bit of a hothead. Still, he's been good to us,

114

no denying that, so we'll have a real celebration when he gets out."

"But it seems like it will go on forever."

"It will pass, Lottie. All things pass. The best thing we can do for Jock and the rest of them is keep things going as best we can." Mabel smiled. "I wish you could have been at the creek, Lottie, to hear the ladies talking about the trial yesterday."

"What happened?"

"I guess it was quite a show. Most of the womenfolk were there, and they all said they hadn't laughed so hard in ages."

"Laughing? At a trial? How? Isn't that against the law or something?"

"Of course it is. What happened was that the judge asked Mrs. Axelson if she was the ringleader of the assembly. She said no, but that she had joined in the singing." Mabel chuckled and clapped her hands together. "You know Mrs. Axelson, Lottie? She doesn't put on any airs, and she sure doesn't dress herself up at all, so I guess the judge thought she was just a mousy little nobody. He asked her if she would sing a verse or two of the song they sang. So she started right in singing."

Charlotte grinned. "Mrs. Axelson has just about the best singing voice you could ever hope to find, doesn't she?"

"Yes. Before you could say 'Jack's your uncle' the whole bunch of them joined in, and the place was packed. They all sang along at the top of their lungs. Everybody laughed, and booed, and applauded—the prisoners, the witnesses, the audience all just kept on singing."

"And then what happened?"

"After that it got pretty serious. The men all pleaded guilty, even if they weren't, because the lawyer told them they would get a lighter sentence that way. Four men were sentenced to two years, and thirty or so got eighteen months hard labour in Oakalla."

"Do you really think the strike is going to help in the long run?"

Mabel shook her head. "Only the good Lord knows the answer to that one. We have to believe it will."

Once the men were in jail, things did improve for the McEwans and their neighbours. As time went on, they came to appreciate having the militia there. There was no longer any danger of riots, the soldiers spent money at the local businesses, and they put on sporting events and other diversions.

The uniform of the the kilties was of great interest to Robbie, as well as to a lot of other people. They gathered at the camp when the sound of bagpipes announced morning reveille to watch men in skirts standing at long tables, stripped to the waist, washing themselves and their clothes.

The army made a great effort to promote goodwill. They held sports afternoons with a band playing to welcome the public, as well as open-air church services with four hundred soldiers in attendance, and pipe-and-drum performances on the Nanaimo waterfront.

They even put on a field day with a mock battle. The army was divided into two sections—the invaders and the defenders. The invaders were to try to enter the "fort," which was the exhibition grounds, and the defenders were to try to stop them any way they could.

Soldiers were still escorting strikebreakers to work,

and there were still a few skirmishes between the striking miners and the strikebreakers, but compared to the violence and bitterness that had shattered the community during the previous weeks, it seemed almost as if life had returned to normal.

Wives and families worried about the prisoners, but those who visited reported that the men were convinced they had done the right thing, and that surely their actions would bring about change eventually.

When Charlotte got home from work one day, there was a letter from Jock sitting on the table. "What does it say?" she asked her mother eagerly.

"Read it yourself, Lottie."

September 18, 1913

Dear Mrs. McEwan and All the Family:

Please excuse the paper. We can only write one letter a week, and the only paper we get is from magazines. One sheet is all we are allowed to send. We also have to leave it open till they read it. We make our own envelopes and porridge is the glue.

I get bread, boiled beef, vegetables, and a cup of water for dinner, and bread, porridge, and black tea for supper.

I am doing fine. The guards treat us pretty well. They say we will be going back home for the trial, which is soon, I think.

Your faithful servant,

Jock

"He sounds all right, don't you think?" Charlotte asked.

"Yes, lass. He's fine."

On the evening of September 19, Charlotte's mother said that Jock, along with the other Extension strikers, had been brought back from Victoria. Many of their wives and families had watched them come off the train handcuffed together.

"They said they all had beards, but they looked healthy enough," Mabel said. "I talked to some of the womenfolk who were there. The men sang as they marched along."

"So they're in the Nanaimo jail now?"

"Yes, but some are going to Oakalla. Eighteen months hard labour."

"Is Jock?"

She nodded. "As far as I could hear."

The very words *Oakalla* and *hard labour* conjured up pictures in Charlotte's mind of chain gangs smashing rocks with sledgehammers and digging ditches by hand for no reason, just for the sake of "hard labour."

But at least he looked healthy, and he was still singing. And he was with his friends. There was something to be said for that. Another consolation was that he would be safe in jail.

🐑

November 30 was Charlotte's birthday. She was sixteen years old. She knew there would be a marble cake with coloured icing and candles, but little did she suspect the surprises that were in store as she walked along the front path after work that day. She could smell roast beef before she even got to the door, and it made her mouth water. She stood in the doorway and looked around.

Robbie and Beatrice were pulling taffy. Danny's cheeks were bulging, and dribbles of sticky saliva were running down his chin. A pint milk bottle set in the middle of the table held an assortment of wild grasses and brightly coloured leaves and berries. Her mother was setting a stack of plates and cutlery beside them.

They were all dressed up. Beatrice was wearing her new pinafore, and Mabel had on a black skirt, a white blouse with a lace collar, and her silver-and-amethyst thistle brooch. Danny and Robbie were both wearing white shirts.

"Whatever in the world?" Charlotte gasped. "Didn't you have supper yet?"

Her mother rushed to greet her, pulled her in, and said, "Lottie, you're sixteen years old. We're having a party."

Charlotte's mouth dropped open, and she looked around in disbelief. There were crepe paper streamers hung across the windows and tacked from the four corners into the centre of the ceiling. A three-layer cake with pink icing and sixteen candles sat on a shelf.

Beatrice laughed and hugged Charlotte's waist, and Danny jumped around like an excited puppy. "I made it myself, Lottie. I made your birthday present special. Hurry up. Get ready for me to give it to you."

"Put on your new dress, Lottie," her mother said.

"Not my new one?" Charlotte asked.

Her mother nodded. "Your new one. This is a special day."

Charlotte carried a basinful of warm water, a wash-cloth, and a towel up to her room and had a sponge bath. Then she undid her braids, combed her hair, tied a pink ribbon around it, and put on her dress with the panels of embroidered eyelet.

TWELVE

When Charlotte came back downstairs, Danny jumped up and grabbed her hand. He pulled her down the last few steps, all the while shoving a package at her. It was wrapped in brown butcher's paper and tied with a piece of white string.

"Happy birthday, Lottie. I made it all myself. Happy birthday."

Charlotte sat on a chair and opened Danny's gift. He had obviously made it himself. "It's lovely, Danny. I like it a whole lot." She bent down to give him a hug. The present was made of two scraps of fabric sewn together, after a fashion. One side was a piece of flannelette left over from his Christmas pajamas, and the other was a scrap left from her dress.

"Do you really? Really and truly?"

"I do, Danny-boy."

"Cross your heart?"

Charlotte made the appropriate gesture. "Cross my heart and hope to die."

"It's a potholder." Her mother mouthed the words silently, waving one of her own potholders behind Danny's back.

"It's the most beautiful potholder in the world," Charlotte said. Danny's face beamed, and he clapped his hands together.

"Come into the sitting room, Charlotte," Beatrice said, pulling her hand.

In the middle of the floor, with a huge crepe paper bow on top, stood a trunk. Charlotte gasped, dropped to her knees beside it, and ran her fingers over the satiny surface. It was made of strips of polished wood, fitted together with wooden pegs. It had leather straps attached with brass fittings and a brass buckle with a lock and a key. She hadn't thought she wanted a trunk, but now that she saw it, she knew that it was the perfect thing.

Charlotte looked up at her mother, who was sitting on the wicker settee, smiling. "Oh, my, it must have cost the world."

"No such thing," Mabel replied briskly. "The Smiths are going back to England. It's time you had a place to keep your good things out of harm's way. Your new dress and so on, and Mrs. Smith sold it for a song."

"I'll bet it cost a song. More like a whole concert!" Charlotte rose and hugged her. "I do love it," she said.

Beatrice tugged at Charlotte's dress. "Open it! Open it!" she said, jumping up and down.

Charlotte undid the buckle and lifted the lid. There

were some tissue-wrapped packages inside, and Beatrice took out the top one and handed it to Charlotte. "I made it."

It was a flour-sack dishtowel, embroiderd on one corner with a bright red rose and shiny green leaves. "For your hope chest," Beatrice said shyly. "Some girls at school said their sisters have hope chests. You can use your trunk for that, can't you?"

"Of course, little sister. Thank you. You did such a fine job of the embroidering, the rose looks real enough to pick."

The next package contained a dress. It was Empire-style—ankle-length, dark blue, high-waisted, with long sleeves, and the cuffs and a Peter Pan collar were made of embroidered white satin.

"Thanks, Mum. You shouldn't have. It all cost too much."

"Not so much, Lottie. Not near as much as you deserve. Just plain wool crepe from the catalogue."

"But the collar and cuffs. They must have taken hours and hours," Charlotte said .

Mabel McEwan dismissed the whole thing as trivial with a wave of her hand. "Open the other package, Lottie."

It was a small teacloth, the kind you would keep for the most special occasions—christenings, or serving tea to ladies. It was made of finely woven linen, hemstitched, and around the border a four-inch band of crochet had been cleverly worked to spell out words:

Some hae meat that canna eat
And some would eat that want it
But we hae meat and we can eat
Sae let the Lord be thankit

Charlotte read the words in a whisper, her voice husky, tears close to the surface. "You brought this from Scotland, didn't you?"

Her mother nodded. "My mother gave it to me."

"But what does it mean?"

"It's an old Scottish grace. And it means that some people have food, but they are sick and not able to eat it, and some people are starving and don't have anything. We are doubly blessed, because we have both good health and food."

There was a knock at the door, and Robbie and Danny raced to answer it. It was Jock. He looked different. He had a black beard, and his face was pale.

"Well, if this isn't a sight for sore eyes," he said, smiling broadly as he looked around the room. "This is my lucky day. I got out just in time to come to the party. "Happy birthday, lass." He pulled off his cap with a flourish and bowed to Charlotte. Then he shook hands with Mabel McEwan, tossed Danny in the air, and lifted Beatrice up and kissed her cheek.

"How come you knew about the birthday?" Danny asked.

Jock winked at Charlotte's mother. "A little bird told me,"

"Do you have to go back to jail?" Danny asked with a worried look. He gripped Jock's hand as he swung his feet off the floor.

"No. I'm out for good."

"But I thought you got eighteen months," Robbie said.

Jock nodded. "I did at first, and they changed it to six months when they found out that some of us had tried to stop the fighting and the torchings. They let us out early at that—because the jails are too crowded."

"Goody, goody," Beatrice exclaimed, jumping up and down and clapping her hands. "Do you want to see me do my drill? Do you like my pinafore? Did you have any parties in jail?"

"Bea, don't be silly," Robbie said in his most dignified manner. "They don't have parties in jail." He turned to Jock. "I've been going to the pithead every day. The guards don't pay no mind to me because I help with the mules, so if you need a spy, I'm your man." He stood straight and squared his shoulders.

Jock slapped Robbie's back. "Right you are, mate. But I smell food!" He rubbed his stomach. "I've been dreaming about home-cooking. Let's have the party and forget about other things for now."

They ate roast beef with potatoes and small onions cooked in the drippings around it; gravy; Yorkshire pudding; carrots and parsnips mashed together; tinned peas; and, for dessert, the birthday cake, each triple-layer slice a swirl of white, pink, green, and chocolate. Nickels and dimes and tiny metal toys—a roller skate, a baby buggy, a ring, a cup, a hat, a ball—magically appeared out of the cake as they cut and began to eat it.

They wouldn't let Charlotte help with the dishes. Mabel washed, Jock and Robbie dried, Beatrice put away, and Danny counted the knives and forks.

While they were washing up, Charlotte sat on the floor in the sitting room and arranged her new blue dress, the teacloth, and her gifts from Beatrice and Danny in her chest to her satisfaction.

They played I Spy, Hide the Thimble, and Button, Button, Who's Got the Button? Danny and Beatrice put on a concert of songs and nursery rhymes, and then they all sang "By the Light of the Silvery Moon," "It's a

Long, Long Way to Tipperary," and "Row, Row, Row Your Boat."

Charlotte was sure that even a princess couldn't have had a better birthday party. And there were more nice things to look foward to. Christmas was just around the corner.

♣

It was Christmas Eve, 1913. Some things had gotten better, some things had gotten worse, and some things were the same as they had been the Christmas before.

One thing that was better was that Santa Claus was coming to the McEwan house for sure.

"I'll help you write a letter, and we'll put it in the fire. The smoke will go up the chimney all the way to the North Pole, and Santa will know what to bring," Charlotte told Danny.

Danny danced around excitedly. "Hurray! You aren't fibbing me, are you? He will bring me what I really, *really* and *truly* want?"

"Well," Charlotte said, hesitating. "I guess the sky's not the limit, but—"

Danny grabbed her hand. "Bend over. I'll whisper so you can write it down. *A train.*"

Charlotte looked alarmed. "I thought you wanted a wagon. That's what you said before."

"I changed my mind," Danny said firmly, crossing his arms on his chest.

"Um, Danny, maybe before we write it down you should think this over."

"I thought it over, and it's a train."

"But you could take a wagon everywhere you go.

Outside even. A train would have to stay indoors all the time, because you wouldn't want to get it muddy. You could haul things in a wagon, and help Mother bring in the kindling wood. What colour wagon would you want if you did get one?"

"I guess red. Write them both down, Charlotte."

"Good idea. Then if Santa Claus has run out of one or the other it won't be a problem."

Charlotte had ordered Danny's wagon from the catalogue a month before, and Jock had hidden it in the Trimbles' attic for safekeeping. He was going to bring it over after Danny went to bed.

Beatrice had asked for a new dress, and the fabric had come from the Timothy Eaton catalogue, too, along with a new doll. Mabel McEwan had done the sewing, and had even made a little dress for the doll to match Beatrice's. They were very pretty, and Charlotte was sure Bea would love them, as well as the six satin hair ribbons the same colours as those in the dresses.

Charlotte had ordered a white shirt and a collar with gold studs for Robbie, but she had already given them to him to wear to the Christmas dance. He had grown so fast that he was practically man-size now, and he was sweet on Sophia's sister, Philomena. Charlotte and her mother both thought it was puppy love, and it would soon wear off, but at least Philomena was a good influence, even though she was only fourteen.

Jock was trying to get Robbie apprenticed to the blacksmith in Wellington. Charlotte prayed he would manage it. She was sure her brother would make a good blacksmith.

The Christmas celebration plans were well in hand. Jock had brought over a big pork roast, and Mabel had made suet pudding, because Jock had said he hadn't had one since he had left Scotland. There was sure to be toffee and shortbread in the brown bundle that had come in the mail from Scotland.

But it wasn't all beer and skittles, as Jock said. Charlotte felt a twinge of guilt when she realized that a lot of the families in Extension would be having the leanest Christmas ever, and here they were having their best one since her father had died. But people on the streets were certainly not feeling sorry for themselves. The carollers were out, and the church bells were ringing. Cheerful shouts filled the night air with "Merry Christmas!" and "God Bless!" It was even snowing.

Jock tapped on the door at 10:00 p.m., and they put the new wagon against the wall behind the tree.

"You will be here for dinner tomorrow, Jock?" Charlotte's mother asked. "I made suet pudding."

"Yes, I will. Thank you, Mrs. McEwan. I wouldn't miss suet pudding for the world, and seeing Danny with his new wagon will be a rare treat. But I'll have to go right after. I have to be in Cumberland the next day."

"Union goings-on, I guess?" Mabel said.

"Yes. It's been a long, hard time, and people are beginning to get sick of it all, but we can't give up. There is a bit of good news. The Vancouver and Nanaimo Coal Company has settled with the miners, and they're back at work in the Jingle Pot mine. But that's just small potatoes.

"It's not just the companies and miners having at each other, don't you see, but the union and the government have got their oars in, too. And, of course, even the miners don't stand together. There's those that are on strike, and others that are strikebreakers.

"Robert Dunsmuir sold out to Canadian Collieries, and he had said he would rather close the mines than be told how he should treat the men. We thought things would be better with Dunsmuir gone, but the Collieries are tarred with the same brush, at least in regard to Extension.

"Did you know that the miners have been trying to get a union going for years? Ten years ago or more nine hundred chaps joined at Extension, and it looked a sure thing. Then the bloody government—excuse my language, but it's just so aggravating. As I was saying, the government outlawed the union. Said it was—" Jock rolled his eyes up as he tried to find the right words "'—revolutionary socialist.' That's what they called it, whatever that means. So the men couldn't do anything about it." He stopped and looked at his hosts, then flushed. "I'm sorry, Mrs. McEwan, Charlotte. I shouldn't be going on like this. It's just, just..."

"I know," Mabel said. "It's dreadfully unfair."

Jock stared at the floor. "Unfair is the least of it."

Mabel made tea and put out scones and blackberry jam. She and Jock talked about Scotland until Charlotte began to nod, and her eyelids drooped. Finally Charlotte climbed wearily up the stairs, but once she was in bed, she couldn't sleep for thinking.

A person couldn't be afraid all the time, she thought. They should be happy when they were able, the way everyone had been at her birthday party. She would remember that day forever, and not just because of the presents. It was being with the people she loved that mattered.

She recalled her father quoting a line he had said was from Tennyson: "'Tis better to have loved and lost than never to have loved at all." He would probably say that he was glad that her mother had married him, and that they had had children to love, even though he was taken away from them when he was only forty.

She wondered if her mother thought that, or did she wish she had stayed an old maid, or got married to someone she didn't love—maybe a minister or a grocery store worker who wasn't likely to be killed at work.

She tried to recapture the bliss she had experienced after the accident when she had been so glad to be alive, when the whole world seemed perfect. It was still the same world, but there were lots of things that weren't perfect, no matter how you looked at it. She hated to admit it, but probably in the end the miners and their families would be no further ahead for all their sacrifices.

But maybe the strike wasn't all a waste. At least there was a big union that the miners could join now, and sooner or later the companies would have to get the message.

Charlotte had thought all she wanted in the world was to get a job so that she could save money and move away from Extension. Then she would be happy. But that idea wasn't all it was cracked up to be, either. She did have some money put by now, and in a couple of years they could probably leave. So what was the problem?

She realized with a jolt that she would miss the little village. She would feel as if she were forsaking the only home she could remember, just because it had seen bad times. Wasn't it the same everywhere? Good times? Bad times?

If they moved away, she would have to leave her father and her sister behind in the cemetery. If she stayed, she would have to do something about her job.

She certainly didn't intend to work at the dynamite plant forever and, anyway, they liked young girls to work there. What would she do when she got older, especially if she was an old maid, which seemed about the likeliest thing at the moment?

A thought popped into her mind that was so tantalizing it made her shiver. What if she could become a school-teacher? No-o-o-o. It would be impossible. She had only finished part of Grade Eight when she had to quit. Besides, it would cost money to go to normal school. When would she have time to study and finish enough grades to get into normal school in the first place? It was impossible! She heard her father's voice: *Nothing is impossible, my little treasure. The impossible just takes longer.*

Maybe it *was* possible. What if she could get lessons to do at home, from the teacher at the school, or in the mail? What if she could spend a half hour studying every workday, and quite a few hours on Sundays and holidays? She could use the money she had saved to pay for going to normal school in Victoria for one year, and then she would be a teacher.

Then she could be an old maid if she felt like it.

Charlotte made a new vow: she would become a teacher. She would stay in Extension and try to make things better. She would teach Danny and the other children how to read and write and do sums so they would be educated. Then they could get better jobs and figure out ways to make changes. The first thing she hoped they would change was the way so many men were killed or crippled in the coal mines.

As she drifted off to sleep, she heard her father say, *Aye, you can do it, lassie.*